*New girl in town . . .*

Ms. Wiggins bustled to her desk. "Of course. You're from New York. We've been expecting you. Your orientation guide will be here to meet you soon."

"Orientation guide?" Julia took a seat.

"Someone to show you around, tell you about school policies, that sort of thing." Ms. Wiggins sniffed.

"Oh." Her old school didn't have any orientation guides. New students marched into the fray alone. It always seemed to work out fine. Was Sullivan High so disorienting that an orientation guide was needed?

"Hi," said a male voice.

Julia's heart leaped. There was no mistaking that voice—low, slow, and sexy. It had to belong to Austin Worth. She looked up, right into his deep, hypnotic eyes. "Hi."

Austin smiled, revealing a dazzling row of white teeth. He looked impossibly crisp and neat in his dark green sweater and knife-creased slacks.

Julia had never found the preppy look to be a turn-on before. Her tastes had always run more to the long-haired, rebellious-looking types with leather jackets and an earring or two. So she couldn't believe how hard her heart was beating as she stared up at the clean-cut guy standing before her. Clearly her taste in guys had changed.

Don't miss any of the books in *Love Stories*
—the romantic series from Bantam Books!

# The Rumor About Julia

## Stephanie Sinclair

BANTAM BOOKS
NEW YORK · TORONTO · LONDON · SYDNEY · AUCKLAND

*For James*

RL 6, age 12 and up

THE RUMOR ABOUT JULIA
*A Bantam Book / November 1997*

*Produced by Daniel Weiss Associates, Inc.*
*33 West 17th Street*
*New York, NY 10011.*
*Cover photography by Michael Segal.*

ISBN: 0-553-49218-7

*Published simultaneously in the United States and Canada*

Bantam Books are published by Bantam Books, a division of Bantam
Doubleday Dell Publishing Group, Inc. Its trademark, consisting of the
words "Bantam Books" and the portrayal of a rooster, is Registered in
U.S. Patent and Trademark Office and in other countries. Marca
Registrada. Bantam Books, 1540 Broadway, New York, New York 10036.

PRINTED IN THE UNITED STATES OF AMERICA

OPM     0 9 8 7 6 5 4 3 2 1

# One

JULIA DRUMMED HER fingers on the steering wheel in time with the music on the radio. Through her car's open window, a warm Indian summer breeze caressed her skin. The sky was an endless sea of azure blue, and the sun lit up everything it touched with its warm, gentle glow.

But Julia still felt miserable. *I think I'm going to be sick, and it's not something I ate either,* she thought. The gigantic knot in her stomach had been tightening steadily, and now it twisted again. She was approaching Sullivan High School as the students were getting out.

Approximately fifteen minutes earlier she had driven into Sullivan, New Jersey, in her vintage clementine orange Volkswagen with a U-Haul rattling along behind. Her heart had continued to sink ever since. This town was to be her new home. *I'll never fit in here,* a voice inside her wailed persistently.

She glanced in the rearview mirror and caught sight of her reflection—three hoop earrings in one ear and none in the other, and a new cranberry streak in her hair. She'd been checking out the kids on the streets, and nobody had streaks in their hair—and earrings came only in twos: one on each lobe.

Usually Julia felt great in her worn-in low-rider jeans, workboots, and her favorite 1970s-style brightly patterned shirt, but today, as she looked around at the kids who were streaming out of the high school, she suddenly felt like she was dressed all wrong for the party. *Oh, where's the chunky jewelry, the platforms, the polyester, the cheesy chic, the funky stuff?* she asked herself each time she drove past another tailored teen.

Here the guys had close-cropped hair that barely brushed the tops of their polo shirts and crewnecks. They wore perfectly pressed khakis and corduroys. Girls wore trendy little outfits that were all so similar that they could have been stamped out of cookie cutters. The clothes, like the cars they drove, screamed money, money, money.

Julia passed the school, coasting by shop after shop with gingerbread trim and window boxes, feeling more and more stressed out. It was all so cute and quaint, and nothing like New York City, where she had lived all of her seventeen years.

Somewhere between Ye Olde Tea Cozy and Grandma's Knitting Basket, she braked at a stoplight. A middle-aged couple looked her over with confused expressions.

"Hi, folks!" She leaned out of the window and flashed them a big friendly smile. The couple barely smiled back.

"Okay, so I don't exactly blend. Do you have to make such a big deal about it?" Julia mumbled to herself. She stepped on the gas. The brake lights on the black BMW in front of her flashed.

*Like, what is your problem, pal?* she asked the driver silently. For blocks the BMW had been all over the place, swerving, speeding up and slowing down. The steady pounding of rock music from the Beemer's radio was practically deafening, and Julia heard bursts of continual wild-and-crazy-guy laughter coming from the car. It was a major pain to be stuck behind such an obnoxious driver, but Julia had other things on her mind.

*My life was firmly in place, and now it's ruined,* she thought. *Stuck waaaaay out here in faaaaar western Jersey. I'll hardly ever be able to get back to New York. I might as well have moved to another planet.*

Homesickness hit her like a punch in the gut. She felt a longing for her friends at "Crate," the High School of Creative Arts. She missed everything about New York: her school; her best friend, Itxey; the apartment she'd shared with her mother in Brooklyn. She even missed the subway.

*The subway? Get a grip, girl,* she told herself. *There's no way anyone rational could miss the subway.*

Without warning, the driver in front of her stopped short. Julia slammed on the brakes and felt the force of the sudden stop send her rocketing forward.

For a frightening moment she thought that her head would strike the windshield.

Julia flung her arm up in front of her eyes and braced herself for the impact. Then the seat belt caught her with a snap and jerked her backward, but not before the steering wheel had dug painfully into her ribs.

The Volkswagen jolted to a stop. Julia was dimly aware that she had just gotten into an accident.

Operating on automatic pilot, she took a deep breath and pulled herself out of the car. All four doors of the BMW opened. Four people, two guys and two girls, got out.

The driver, a stocky, muscular guy with short sandy brown hair and squinty gray eyes, started shouting at Julia immediately. "You jerk! Where did you learn how to drive? Look what you did to my car!" he yelled, gesturing to his BMW with a thick, stubby finger.

Julia looked in the direction he was pointing and was relieved to see that the extent of the damage was only a dented fender. Then she bent down and quickly examined the fender of her VW, breathing a sigh of relief. There wasn't a scratch on it.

"If you hadn't stopped so quickly, this wouldn't have happened," she murmured as she straightened up.

The guy went ballistic. "What?" he shouted. "*You're* the one who smashed *my* fender. I can't believe you've got the nerve to try to blame me—to try to make me look bad!" His face was getting so red that he looked like he was either going to pass out or have a major heart attack.

Julia blinked. *This guy needs a reality check for sure.*

"I wasn't trying to make you look bad," she said slowly and calmly in her most adult voice. "I was simply stating a fact. If you *hadn't* slammed on the brakes, if you had given me the *slightest* warning you were going to stop, this wouldn't have happened." She paused, raking her fingers through her thick, shoulder-length brown hair. "I'll be glad to fix your car myself—for free, of course."

The boy narrowed his eyes and curled his lip scornfully. "I'm sure you know a lot about auto body repair," he said, his voice dripping with sarcasm. He rolled his eyes and glanced at his friends.

"A lot more than *you* know about driving," Julia retorted, smiling with exaggerated sweetness.

His three friends chuckled a bit, and the guy suddenly turned to them. "Are you guys laughing at me?" he snapped.

Instantly, his friends stopped laughing. The boy turned back to Julia. "You must be crazy to think I'd let you get your hands on my car. It's not a clownmobile like that piece of junk you're riding around in."

The guy put both hands in his back pockets and looked at Julia as if he were just noticing her for the first time. He gave her a slow once-over and did an elaborate double take. "You've made a real interesting selection in wardrobe. Nice streak of colored hair too. You think you're cool because you're different?"

Julia ground the heel of her boot into the asphalt.

She took a deep breath and exhaled in a short burst. "Look," she said, "when you're done having fun, we can exchange insurance information and get on with our lives, okay?"

"I can get back to my life, and you can get back to the circus, is that it?"

"Hey, Lucas, chill out, man. You're way out of line. It's a little dent in your fender, that's all. It'll cost a few hundred to fix. Relax." The words came from the other guy who had gotten out of the car. He stood on the periphery of the group.

The guy whose name was Lucas shot his friend a look. He hesitated a moment, his eyes wavering uncertainly. Then he walked away, fists clenched at his sides. "Just forget the insurance stuff. I've got the money to get it fixed," he called over his shoulder.

Julia looked after him in stunned silence. She was about to give the other guy a grateful glance when she realized that her art supplies were laying all over the street. She cringed.

Evidently the door of the U-Haul had popped open when she stopped so suddenly. The toolbox she used to store her charcoal and brushes had exploded. Canvases were strewn everywhere.

"Oh, no," she groaned softly. "Why me? Why me?" Horns were honking all around. Julia ran to the back of the U-Haul.

A can of red paint had broken open and splashed all over. Before she realized what was happening, Julia stepped in a slippery paint puddle and her heels slipped out from under her.

It seemed to her that it was all happening in slow motion. She knew she was falling, but she was powerless to stop it. The scene replayed itself in her mind several times, *splat! splat! splat!*, before she actually, *splat!*, hit the ground, landing in the middle of the puddle of paint.

A chorus of giggles and guffaws reached her ears. Lucas and his friends were laughing at her.

Julia gritted her teeth. *At least all that's hurt is my dignity.* She managed to pull herself to her feet and reach for a canvas, leaving a bloodred handprint on its surface.

She was covered with paint—her arms, her hair—she had even managed to get paint on her legs, through the holes in her jeans.

*What else can go wrong?* Julia took a deep breath and told herself to keep calm. There was no use in getting stressed out. Ignoring the honking horns and the sounds of laughter, Julia opened the VW's trunk, got out a rag, and went to work wiping off the paint. The horn honkers started to detour around her.

"Sorry that my friend was out of control," a male voice apologized from above. "He loses his temper easily. Can I help you pick up your things?"

"Sure," Julia responded without looking up. "Thanks."

She tried to rub the paint off her arms, but wiping just left long red streaks and splotches on her skin instead. Paint squished and oozed between her fingers and under her jeans. The rag was soaked.

7

"I guess that's the best I can do," Julia muttered with a sigh. She tossed the grungy rag in the trunk and went to repack the U-Haul.

There was nothing left to pick up. "I put everything back and made sure the door was locked," the guy said from behind her. "You'll have to clean some stuff up, but basically there's no harm done." The sound of his deep voice suddenly sent a little chill racing up Julia's spine. She had been too preoccupied before to notice how smooth and sexy it was.

Julia turned to face him, then had one of those experiences she'd only read about or seen in the movies. The sight of him made her breath catch in her throat.

He was smiling at her. It was a smile that was a mixture of arrogance, mischief, and a charming hint of shyness. A lock of short dark hair curled over his forehead.

But what affected Julia most were his eyes. They were the deepest, darkest brown she had ever seen.

Those eyes were looking into her own with a piercing, penetrating gaze. The intensity made her feel off balance, like she needed to look away.

But all she could do was stare back at him. Even though she felt a dull red flush flaming into her cheeks, she still couldn't turn away. He didn't move either. They both just stood there looking at each other.

"You ought to take those jeans off before you get back in the car," he finally said, still smiling. "You'll get paint all over the seat."

Julia heard the teasing note in his voice and

couldn't resist a smile herself. Especially since he was so gorgeous. "Right," she said. "I'll just take off my pants right here in the street."

The guy's sexy smile widened. "It's just a suggestion."

"Austin! Austin!" A girl's shrill voice suddenly cut through the air. The spell was broken.

The guy blinked, as if he too had just come out of a trance. "Just a minute, Courtney," he said, looking over his shoulder at one of the blond girls who had gotten out of Lucas's car. "You guys go ahead. I'll be right there."

He turned back to Julia, his eyes sparkling. Now his smile was barely there, just a corner of his mouth turned up, making him look terribly masculine and sexy and boyish all at the same time. "You're blushing," he said.

*Yes, I am,* Julia realized, and wished she could hide her face in her hands. Instead, she gave her hair a toss and tried to pretend she hadn't heard him. "I'll put a towel down on the seat to protect it from the paint. That way, I can keep my pants on," she said.

"That's too bad." The boy's mischievous smile flashed again.

*Very smooth, Julia, talking about keeping your pants on.* Julia could feel the red in her cheeks deepening.

The boy didn't take his eyes off her. He held out his hand. "I'm Austin Worth."

"Julia Marin." Julia stuck out her hand too, but drew it back when she saw that the red paint had

9

even gotten underneath her nails. She looked up at Austin, and they both laughed. Julia felt warm inside. Electrified. Even the air around her felt like it was charged with their mutual attraction.

"I haven't seen you around. I'll take a wild guess and say the U-Haul means you're moving," Austin said.

Julia felt his voice flow over her. "Yes, I'm moving here—to Sullivan." She kept looking into his eyes. "I'll be going to Sullivan High."

"The only high school here."

"Austin! Come on!" This time, the girl sounded like she was on the verge of a hissy fit.

Austin touched Julia's arm lightly. "Well, I gotta go. See you."

His brief touch sent a little shower of sparks through Julia. She felt a lump forming in her throat as she watched him go. She realized she was trembling. Julia got back in the car, a tumbling mass of confusion inside.

A shiver went through her body. For a few incredible, miraculous moments, Austin Worth had made Julia feel like she could fall in love.

# Two

JULIA GAVE THE painting a final brush stroke and stood back to examine her work. She had created a picture of her dream guy. He was perfect . . . handsome, sexy, and charming. She gazed at the picture, losing herself in his penetrating stare.

Then her dream guy stepped out of the canvas and reached out for her hand. He gave her a small smile. "Welcome to Sullivan," he said.

He then leaned in to kiss her. He brushed Julia's hair away from her face and put his lips on hers, kissing her passionately and deeply. But instead of being wonderful, it was like kissing a pillowcase.

Julia's eyelids jerked open, and she spat out a mouthful of cotton fabric. *That's because it is a pillowcase!* Her mouth felt as dry as dust. *I must have been kissing that pillowcase a long time,* she thought.

The image of Austin Worth's face floated before her. He was the guy in her dream.

What a way to start the morning. Julia sat up and brushed her tangled hair off of her forehead. She shoved her feet into her Chinese silk slippers and pulled on a blue bathrobe adorned with huge green stars. For a moment, she sat on the edge of her bed looking at her new room and wishing she could make sense of the feelings that were tumbling around inside her.

The phone rang, startling Julia so much that she jumped. *This guy has me so rattled, I'm a bundle of nerves.* "Hello?" she answered.

"Hey, girl, how's it going?"

"Itxey!" A smile spread over Julia's face. "Your timing's perfect! I really need to talk."

"Wow, you're all wound up, and it's only eight." As usual, Itxey's voice crackled with excitement. "I thought I might wake you, but I couldn't wait to call. Tell me about the place—what's it like there?"

"Oh my gosh, you wouldn't believe it, Itx. It's jock city. Guys in khakis and crewnecks, girls in little outfits that cost a fortune." She threw herself back against the pillows. "People were actually staring at my car—and at me—as I drove through the streets."

Itxey laughed lightly. "Well, at least you stand out." She paused and then asked more seriously, "Is it really that horrible there?"

Julia shrugged. "I don't know. I'll get a better feel for the place when I go to school." She twirled the sash of her robe. "I ran into some people, literally, when I collided with a car, and I met a guy—"

"What guy?" Itxey interrupted. "The guy you ran into?"

"No. Another guy in the car. His name's Austin." Julia stopped talking abruptly. She wasn't sure what to say next.

"What's he like?" Itxey prompted.

Julia sat up straighter. "Oh, he seemed nice, that's all. Really good-looking. *Great* looking. His friends were obnoxious, but he was something else."

"Something else," Itxey echoed. "Julia, could you elaborate on that, please?"

Julia chewed her lower lip. "Well, he wasn't rude, for one thing. He seemed . . . interesting. I don't know, I don't even know the guy, but I sort of felt like I do. . . ." Julia's voice trailed off.

"Aha," Itxey said knowingly. "Don't tell me you finally have a crush on somebody?"

"What makes you think I have a crush on him? I don't get crushes."

Itxey didn't miss a beat. "Yeah, yeah. The Julia Marin no-nonsense approach to romance. Well, you can't fool me. I can hear it in your voice. You took one look at this guy and fell for him. He made your heart beat a mile a minute, and you can't stop thinking about him. Tell me it's true! Please!"

Julia couldn't help laughing. "Okay, okay, you've got the general idea. But I'm not going to get carried away—"

"No!" Itxey cut her off. "*Get* carried away, Julia. Take a chance. If you run into this guy around

13

school, just see what develops without holding back so much."

Julia blinked. "Huh?"

"If you like him and you find yourself falling for him, let it happen. You're always so cautious. Like with Zeke, always holding him at arm's length."

Julia let out a long sigh. She had to admit that was true. Zeke had been her boyfriend for nearly a year back in New York. When they said their good-byes, he said he had never really felt close to her.

"Itxey, things with Zeke never clicked. We just weren't right for each other."

"You really think so, Jule?" Itxey asked. "You really don't mind not seeing him anymore?"

Julia twisted the telephone cord. "No, even though I probably should. It's over anyway."

There was a moment of silence on the other end of the line. "Give this guy a chance," Itxey said. "Anyway, I gotta go. I'm starting that pottery class this morning, learning to use the wheel and all."

"Okay. I wish I were going with you," Julia said.

"Me too. Call me. 'Bye."

Julia heard the click as Itxey hung up. Then she closed her eyes and let herself relive every detail of her first meeting with Austin. She could feel the exquisite shiver that the brief touch of his hand had sent through her body.

She opened her eyes. *Why can't I get him out of my mind?* she wondered with exasperation. She flung her pillow on the floor and headed downstairs.

Julia padded into the small room off the kitchen

that was to be her art studio. Morning sunlight streamed through the large windows on three of the four walls. Outside was a view of the yard, which sloped down to a small pond.

*Working here will be better than painting in the corner of my room and going to sleep amid turpentine fumes,* she admitted. *But I'd give this studio up in a heartbeat for a chance to go back to New York.*

She began to arrange her canvases and supplies. Thoughts of Austin Worth kept popping into her mind just as fast as she tried to push them away.

"You're up awfully early."

Julia whirled around. Her mother was standing in the doorway, holding out a mug of coffee. She was wrapped in a huge terrycloth robe, and her light brown hair was pulled back in a ponytail.

"Thanks," Julia murmured as she accepted the mug. "I wanted to put the studio together."

Her mother stood in the center of the room and did a three-hundred-and-sixty degree turn.

"You're off to a good start organizing. I think you're going to love working in here. I hope it makes leaving New York easier." Her mother pressed her lips into a tight, guilty line and shook her head. "You know I just couldn't pass up this job. If I could've found something better in New York . . ."

Julia walked over and put an arm around her mother's shoulders. "I know, Mom," she said. "I told you, I'll make the best of the situation. I'm going back to New York next year anyway. I'll just chalk this year up as experience."

Julia watched her words erase the cramped, apologetic look from her mother's face. "I'm so proud of you." Her mother's eyes became watery as she spoke. "You've been so mature about this move. And driving up here on your own yesterday so that I could get settled in here early . . ." Her mother's voice trailed off. She shook her head. "When did you get so grown-up?"

Julia smiled. "I don't know, Mom. But enough with the sentimental stuff for now."

Her mother laughed, taking Julia's arm in hers as the two of them walked into the kitchen and sat down at the pine table. Julia crossed her legs and tucked her robe around them. Gizmo, their old gray cat, leaped onto her lap.

"I'm going to look for a part-time job today."

Her mother raised an eyebrow. "You're not wasting any time. What do you have in mind? A waitressing job at the local hangout, maybe? You'd get to meet people and wear a cute uniform."

Julia looked up sharply. "Are you kidding?" she asked. Her mother smiled back. Then they both burst out laughing.

Julia's one and only waitressing job had been a disaster. She had ended up pouring a pitcher of ice water in the lap of a rude customer. Her entire employment had lasted all of two hours.

"You know very well what kind of job I'm going to look for. I saw the perfect place too. Max's Garage. I drove past there yesterday; it's just outside the main part of town. It looks like an old-fashioned

16

garage. Just like the one Dad used to have."

Julia bit her lip. She wished she hadn't mentioned her father. Her mother acted as if nothing were wrong, but Julia could see the sudden sadness in her eyes.

"Anyway," Julia hurried on, "I hope they need someone. I'm ready for my usual battle about being a girl and knowing my way around cars."

Julia's mother smiled knowingly. "As soon as you open your mouth, there won't be any doubt."

"I know," Julia said with a sigh. "I just wish I didn't have to go through the drill every time." She carried her coffee cup to the sink. "I better get going."

Twenty minutes later she pulled her VW to a stop in front of Max's Garage. Except for the brand-new gas pumps that stood out front, the place looked like it had been frozen in time. Attached to the garage was a low, ramshackle building. There was a faded tan and red sign mounted over what looked like the office—a small cluttered room with dusty old-fashioned venetian blinds on the window.

Through the open double doors of the garage, Julia could see a man in mechanic's overalls peering into an auto engine. She couldn't see his face, but she got a glimpse of his hair, which was short and sprinkled with gray.

When she got out of the car, a younger, dark-haired man who also wore a mechanic's uniform approached her. He looked like he was in his mid-twenties. "Can I help you?" he asked.

"I'm looking for Max. Is that you?"

"No, I'm Tony. Max is my dad." Tony gestured toward the man in the garage who was bent over the engine. Then he looked back at her with questioning green eyes.

*Here we go,* thought Julia. She cleared her throat. "I'm looking for a job."

Tony shifted a wrench from one hand to the other and back again. "Hmmm . . . okay. I'll get my dad to talk to you." He trotted off.

After a moment Max walked up to her. He held out a powerful and calloused hand to Julia. "I'm Max Wetherby," he said in a gravelly voice.

"Julia Marin."

The man looked at her and said simply, "Yes?"

"I just moved into town, and I'm looking for a job."

Julia waited for the lady-you've-got-to-be-kidding-me look, but Max didn't change his expression. "My son keeps bugging me to hire some part-time help. Says I'm working too hard." Max shrugged. "But I feel fine." He paused for a moment. "You know your way around cars? I'm not just talking about pumping gas."

"If you're talking oil changes, tune-ups, that sort of thing, I can handle it."

The man stroked his chin thoughtfully. "Is that so. . . ." It was more of a statement than a question.

"Come with me," he said, leading her into the garage. He gestured to a slightly beat-up blue sedan with the hood raised. "A customer brought this in complaining about a 'funny noise.'"

18

"Let me guess," said Julia. "They want you to make the *zonk, zonk, zonk* go away."

Max chuckled. "A whistling noise, actually. What would you do?"

Julia folded her arms. "Did they say when they heard the noise? On a smooth road? Only when the car went over a bump? When they started the engine, or only when the car was moving?"

"All the time," Max replied.

Julia peered into the engine. After a moment she smiled. "This is an easy one," she said. "This fan belt is shot."

Max nodded. "You're right." He walked over to the wall where a jumble of parts in boxes were stacked on ancient metal shelves. He picked out a new fan belt and handed it to Julia. "Want to try changing it?"

"You bet," Julia told him. She looked around and quickly located the right tools. Then she went to work loosening the fan. With a few deft motions, she slid the old belt off and replaced it with the new one. She then slid the fan back in and tightened the screws that held it in place.

Max examined her work and flashed her a smile. "Where'd you learn so much about cars?"

"From my dad," Julia said in a tight voice.

"Seems he taught you well. You can wash up over there." He gestured toward the sink.

Julia barely glanced at the streak of grease on her palm. "Do I get the job?" she asked.

"I'll think about it." He turned and walked out front.

As soon as he was gone, Tony walked into the garage. "How'd it go?" he asked.

"I'm not sure." Julia turned on the faucet and scrubbed at the grease spot. "He's thinking."

Tony's green eyes lit up in his boyish face. "He sizes up people like *that*," he told her, snapping his fingers. "He wouldn't have given you a tryout if he didn't have a feeling you had potential," he said. "He'll give you the job. Trust me." He gave her a good-natured pat on the shoulder and turned toward the office.

"I hope you're right," Julia called after him. She looked out front as she dried her hands on a stiff paper towel. Two cars were driving up. She drew her breath in sharply. One was a burgundy Camaro. The other was a black Beemer . . . with a dented fender.

Sure enough, Lucas, the guy she'd had the run-in with the day before, got out of the BMW. Then her heart jumped: The driver of the burgundy Camaro was none other than Austin Worth. The guys started talking to Max.

Julia took a deep breath and walked out front.

Lucas's mouth dropped open when he saw her. Austin, however, broke into a wide grin.

"Julia, Lucas here has gone and dented his fender," Max said, his tone businesslike. "Have you ever done any auto body repair work?"

Julia kept her eyes on Max and nodded.

"Okay, then," Max went on, "how would you fix this?"

Julia swallowed and pushed a wayward piece of hair off her face. "First, I'd bang out the dent with a hammer. Then I'd use a body puller. I'd fill it in with the body puller and sand—maybe I'd do it twice. I think that would be enough for this dent, since it's not bad."

"Hey, Max, what's going on here?" Lucas interrupted. "Are you using my car for some auto repair school test?"

"Shhh!" Max commanded. "Julia, go on."

"Uh, okay." Julia collected her breath again. "I'd follow it up with red lead to smooth out the blemishes in the body filler, do a couple coats or so of that, and follow up each coat with sanding. Then I'd sand the paint off the whole fender and prime it, followed by maybe three coats of alternate paint and sanding."

Max was nodding as she spoke. "You're right on the money. Tell you what—you're hired. We'll just have to work out your schedule. This fender will be your first job."

Julia smiled gratefully. She looked over at Lucas. His face had turned red with anger, just as it had the day before.

"No way, no way she's going to get her hands on my car!" he sputtered.

Max jutted out his chin defiantly. "Listen, Lucas. This is my shop, and I run it the way I want. I decide who I'm going to employ and what they're going to do. Got it? So if you don't like the way things are done here, take your car elsewhere."

21

Lucas acted as if he hadn't heard a word. "I said no way!" He opened his mouth to say more, but Austin cut him off.

"Calm down, Lucas."

Lucas's mouth was still hanging open. He drew back as if he had been slapped.

"Come on," Austin urged. "Max knows what he's doing. He stands behind his work."

Lucas looked from Max to Austin with uncertainty. "Okay, okay," he said grudgingly. "I'll let my car be part of auto repair school."

"It's all settled then." Max brought his hands together in a single loud clap. "Lucas, let's go into the office. I'll draw up the paperwork."

Max started walking toward the office, Lucas on his heels. But Austin stayed where he was.

"Hey, Austin, c'mon," Lucas called when he realized Austin was lagging behind.

"No, you go ahead," Austin answered, his eyes drifting over Julia. "I'll wait here."

Lucas hesitated for a moment, knitting his brows. Then he suddenly whirled around and followed Max.

Julia and Austin stood looking at each other in silence. Julia felt her heart flutter in a replay of all the sensations that she had felt when she had first stared into Austin's eyes the day before.

*Do you kiss as good as you look?* she couldn't help wondering. She was just thankful he couldn't read her mind.

Austin tucked one thumb in his belt loop and

walked over to Julia's Volkswagen. "So, what do you call that color?" he asked.

"Clementine orange." Julia was glad to talk about her car. Being in familiar territory would help calm the butterflies that were starting to flutter in her stomach. "They started making it in 1971. This is a '72, though. It was tough finding someone who could match the color perfectly."

"I'll bet," Austin said. "Lot of problems keeping it running?"

"No, not a lot. Things do come up from time to time. . . ." Julia's voice trailed off. She was having trouble maintaining the power of speech as Austin studied the car and moved closer and closer to her at the same time. Soon he was so close that his sleeve brushed hers. And then he edged even closer, still looking at the car.

"You see these vents in the hood in the back, over the engine?" she asked him, not moving an inch. She had to concentrate on keeping her voice steady. "Water gets in through them when it rains, and then the engine gets wet, especially near the distributor coil, and the distributor can short out. You have to dry off the coil, pull out the wire, dry it off, and put it back." Julia paused. *I'm rambling on and on,* she thought.

But Austin was gazing at her with rapt attention. "You really know what you're doing." His deep brown eyes took on a mischievous sparkle. "You must be good with your hands."

Julia felt her cheeks get hot. She was trying to think of a smart response when Lucas emerged from the office. "C'mon, Austin, let's go." He tapped his watch. "We'll be late." He got into Austin's Camaro.

Austin glanced over his shoulder at Lucas, then looked back at Julia. "We're supposed to meet some friends," he explained. He looked into Julia's eyes for a moment, making her heart flutter all over again.

"See you," Julia said to Austin's back as he walked away. She suddenly felt off balance. She had definitely felt a charged connection with Austin. It was just too bad it had been abruptly broken by Lucas.

"I sure hope that girl knows what she's doing around cars," Lucas muttered as they drove away from the garage.

"I bet that girl knows what she's doing, period," Austin said, smiling. An image of Julia's face floated before his mind's eye. He glanced at Lucas and saw that he was staring at him. "Why are you looking at me like that?" he asked.

"You were *hitting* on the girl who *hit* my car," Lucas said.

Austin raised his eyebrows. "What's your point?"

Lucas shook his head. "I'm just saying you seem interested in a major way. I've never seen you like that over a girl before."

Austin's smile widened. "You might be right. There just might be something special about that girl."

"Maybe," Lucas responded. "But how can you be so sure? You just met her. I think you should slow down."

Austin frowned, stopping at a traffic light. "Why?"

Lucas hesitated. "I can't put my finger on it. There's something about her, though. She seems like the kind of girl who likes to party." He popped a piece of gum in his mouth. "I think the girl gets around."

Austin snorted. "'Gets around? Likes to party?' What are you talking about? You don't know anything about this girl, Lucas. You're not making sense."

"I'm just calling it how I see it," Lucas responded icily.

Austin didn't reply. He just looked ahead at the road, his lips pressed in a thin line. Lucas's immaturity was getting to him—he could be so shallow sometimes. Austin had had enough of this conversation.

After a few moments of silence, Austin saw Lucas slump back into his seat angrily. *Why am I defending a girl I hardly know?* Austin wondered.

He braked at a stop sign. *Face it,* he told himself, *she's gotten under your skin.*

Like no girl ever had.

# Three

"HEY! HOW WAS your weekend?"
    "Love your hair!"
"He said *what?*"

It was Monday morning, and Julia was swept into the tide of bodies that surged through Sullivan High's main hallway. She had never felt more like an outsider. She could pinpoint the exact moment when the feeling had started: right when she walked through the front door of the school. Carpeting! Who ever heard of a high school with carpeted halls? No wonder the place was so quiet.

At Crate the ancient hallways were like echo chambers. Julia would have done anything to be surrounded by the whir of the pottery wheel, the tuning of instruments, and the chatter of classmates on their way to drama class.

Julia took a deep breath. Nothing but freshly shampooed carpets. It made her long for the comforting

26

aromas of clay, turpentine, and linseed oil to which she was accustomed. She wanted to see someone lugging one of their own unusual pieces of art. Here nobody carried anything more exotic than a laptop. "Ohhh!" Julia said as someone slammed into her, knocking her off balance.

"Sorry, I slipped," said a girl in a red miniskirt.

"It's okay. No harm done." Julia smiled. Then she felt a prickle of annoyance as Ms. Red Miniskirt looked Julia up and down coolly, giving her a once-over.

"What do you call that lipstick?" the girl asked.

"Grape Candy."

"Hmmm . . . creepy." The girl puckered her lips as if she'd just bit into something sour. Then she sauntered away down the hall. Julia's eyes flashed as she looked after her. *Thanks for the warm welcome,* chica.

With a sigh Julia pushed open the door to the school office. Two white-haired ladies behind the desk broke off their conversation at once and stared at her, looking so startled that Julia almost laughed. *I guess I do clash with everybody else here,* she thought. No one was wearing anything that remotely resembled her vintage purple minidress with bell sleeves.

"Ahem!" The lady who was wearing her glasses on a cord around her neck cleared her throat. "What can I do for you, dear?"

"I'm Julia Marin. I'm here to register for classes." She read the name tag fastened to the

27

woman's beige sweater and added, "Ms. Wiggins."

Ms. Wiggins bustled to her desk and punched some keys on her computer. "Of course. You're from New York. We've been expecting you." She handed Julia a clipboard with several forms attached to it. "Here, take this and sit over there," she said, pointing to a bench. "Make sure you fill in all the blanks. Your orientation guide will be here to meet you soon."

"Orientation guide?" Julia took a seat.

"Someone to show you around, tell you about school policies, that sort of thing," Ms. Wiggins sniffed.

"Oh." Julia picked up the pen that was attached to the clipboard by a squiggly little wire. Her old school didn't have any orientation guides. New students marched into the fray alone. It always seemed to work out fine. Was Sullivan High so disorienting that an orientation guide was needed?

She concentrated on filling out the forms. The information they asked was pretty routine: list previous schools, areas of interest, next of kin, basic information.

"Hi," said a male voice.

Julia's heart leaped. There was no mistaking that voice—low, slow, and sexy. It had to belong to Austin Worth. She looked up, right into his deep, hypnotic eyes. "Hi."

Austin smiled, revealing a dazzling row of white teeth. He looked impossibly crisp and neat in his dark green sweater and knife-creased slacks.

Julia had never found the preppy look to be a

turn-on before. Her tastes had always run more to the long-haired, rebellious-looking types with leather jackets and an earring or two. So she couldn't believe how hard her heart was beating as she stared up at the clean-cut guy standing before her. Clearly her taste in guys had changed.

"Nice dress," he commented.

"It's really old." Julia had said the first words that popped into her mind and instantly wanted to reach out and grab them back. *What a brilliant comment, Julia,* whispered a voice inside her head.

She felt even more embarrassed when she noticed that her dress had ridden halfway up her thighs. She tried to tug it down without being obvious.

Austin glanced at her legs briefly, then looked away. He sat down on the bench beside her. As he did, his thigh brushed against hers, sending a surge of warmth through her entire body. "So, what brings you to Sullivan in the first place?" Austin asked.

It couldn't have been a more ordinary question, but coming from Austin, it sounded beyond charming to Julia.

"My mother got a great job offer," Julia said as she continued to tug on her skirt. "She would have stayed in New York if I had thrown a fit, but I just couldn't do that to her."

"I'm glad you didn't," Austin said slowly.

Julia felt herself free-falling for him. *Oh, knight in shining armor—or, rather, hundred percent wool—make me your princess.* She had a quick vision of him carrying her through the halls of Sullivan and out the door to his chariot, the burgundy Camaro.

Suddenly a voice cut in, and the blissful fantasy vanished. "Well, it looks as if you already met someone at Sullivan. As a matter of fact, it looks like you two know each other pretty well." The voice belonged to a gorgeous African American girl with huge eyes and a delicate oval face.

"I'm Kayla Phillips," she said. "I'll be your orientation guide." She held out a slim, manicured hand. Julia shook it numbly, still in a daze.

Kayla clearly took more fashion chances than the other girls at Sullivan. She was wearing chunky maroon pumps with ankle straps, flare-legged pants, and a sweater with neon stripes. *Not too funky, but not blah either,* thought Julia. *Unique. Sophisticated.* She noticed that Kayla carried a copy of *Vogue* on top of her notebook.

"Julia, I'll just be a minute. I've got to get a handbook and some other stuff." Kayla disappeared behind the desk.

Austin grinned at Julia. They both stood up. "It looks like we know each other pretty well, huh? Let's make it real. How about lunch today?"

"Love to!" Julia blurted out, and then immediately regretted responding with such enthusiasm. *I might as well have jumped up and clapped my hands.*

Austin's lips twitched. "Terrific. My friends and

I sit at the round table in the corner by the windows. You can't miss us."

"Huh?"

Much to Julia's dismay, Austin repeated directions to his table in the cafeteria. She had been picturing a romantic table for two at some cozy little bistro. *Don't people at Sullivan know you're only supposed to eat in the cafeteria when the weather's lousy?* "Uh, that sounds great. I'll see you at lunch, then."

Austin turned to walk away, then stopped. "I can't believe what I almost did." He shook his head. "I came to pick up the mail for the school paper. Then I started talking to you, and I almost forgot why I was here." He flashed Julia a dazzling smile. "Well, it's no wonder," he added with a wink.

The compliment warmed Julia right to her bones. Before she could think of anything to say back to him, Austin grabbed some papers from one of the mailboxes on the wall. "I'll see you later," he told her.

"Okay," Julia murmured. She never thought a guy could look sexy in wool, but Austin sure did. She was still staring at his back when Kayla thrust a manila envelope into her hands. "Here's your handbook and gym manual and some other stuff you can have fun reading tonight. If you can get your mind off Austin Worth long enough, that is."

Julia felt herself blushing. "It's not like that."

"Whatever you say." Kayla gave Julia a knowing look. "Okay, I'll show you around. You'll miss homeroom and your first class today because of the grand tour. Let's get started."

Julia followed Kayla out of the office. There was something vaguely familiar about her. She kept stealing glances at the girl, trying to figure out what it was.

"Do I have something stuck between my teeth, or what?" Kayla asked finally.

Julia shook her head quickly. "I didn't mean to stare," she said. "It's just that there's something about you . . ."

"I look like Ali Phillips, maybe? He's my twin brother."

"Unbelievable!" Julia exclaimed. Everyone knew who Ali Phillips was. He was an Olympic gymnastic hopeful. Magazines had done so many interviews with the handsome young athlete that he was as much a celebrity as Brad Pitt. "*That's* why you look familiar; you look just like him. Are you into gymnastics too?"

"For fun only. Ali's away in Colorado where there's a training camp. He has to travel all the time too, to go to meets. It's all work and no play, but he loves it." Kayla fingered her copy of *Vogue*. "Fashion design is my thing. I'm going to study it in New York next year. What about you?"

Common thread discovered, the two girls jabbered away.

"They didn't tell me you went to the High School of Creative Arts!" Kayla exclaimed as they headed toward the gym. "I'm jealous!"

"It's pretty cool there," Julia said, beaming. "It's tough switching senior year. But I'll be back in

New York in the fall. I'm going to Pratt Institute in Brooklyn. That's where I live—I mean, where I lived."

Kayla eyes grew wide. "I'm going to go to F.I.T. in Manhattan. Have you heard of it?"

"The Fashion Institute of Technology? Of course!"

"You'll have to fill me in on the best places to go," Kayla told her. "Like where to get the best burritos and where to go dancing."

Julia grinned. "I think I can manage that."

"And you'll have to tell me where to get a dress like yours," Kayla said admiringly. "It's totally cool."

Julia raised her eyebrows. "Thanks. I don't think most people here share your opinion, though."

Kayla waved her hand dismissively. "Never mind. Sullivan isn't exactly the place for cutting-edge fashion, if you know what I mean."

Julia laughed, grateful to finally meet somebody to whom she could relate. She suddenly felt a lot more positive about Sullivan High.

*It won't be so bad here, after all,* Julia told herself as she scanned the cafeteria at lunch looking for Austin. She saw the round table in the corner of the room, but no one was there.

It had been a while since Julia had eaten in a school cafeteria. Since last year's blizzard had kept everyone indoors at Crate, to be exact.

This was like no cafeteria she'd ever seen,

though. Like the halls, it too was carpeted. There were bold-striped curtains on the windows, and the rectangular tables were placed at angles instead of the normal school cafeteria end-to-end army barrack style. Round tables were placed here and there in between. There was even a CD jukebox.

Julia grabbed a tray and stood in line. As she slid her tray along, she couldn't believe that there weren't the obligatory cafeteria globs of mashed potatoes drowned in lumpy gravy. No spaghetti stuck together with gluey sauce. No peas.

"Hamburger?" asked a man behind the counter.

Julia nodded.

"Rare, medium, or well done?"

"Medium, please," Julia told him. The place was like a restaurant. She realized that it didn't even have that cafeteria smell—that universal yucky food odor.

Julia emerged from the lunch line clutching her tray and her books. She looked over to the table in the corner, and this time, Austin was there. Unfortunately, so was Lucas.

"Hi, Julia." Austin got to his feet when Julia arrived and pulled a chair out for her.

"You know Lucas," he said. "And this is Courtney." Julia recognized the blond girl as one of Lucas's passengers from the other day.

"Hi, Courtney."

Courtney gave Julia a frosty smile. Julia was introduced to another guy, Gavin, a redheaded jock type, and two other girls, Tiffany and Amber. They both looked pretty much like Courtney clones. The three girls were all wearing variations of sweater sets and tailored pants or skirts. Today Courtney was wearing a hat adorned with a clump of holly berries.

"I'm surprised I didn't see you in the lunch line," Julia said to them. "The food here looks great."

Courtney's fork stopped in midair. "You went through the *line?* That food is *gross. We* always go over to the International Food Court." She eyed the food on Julia's plate with obvious distaste. Then she shrugged. "Oh well, I guess you didn't know any better."

The bite of burger Julia had just swallowed stuck in her throat. "Thanks for the tip," she said tightly.

"The International Food Court is over on the other side. They have different dishes every day, sometimes Mexican, sometimes Chinese, Japanese, you name it. I should have told you," Austin said.

"No problem." Before Julia could say another word to Austin, Lucas tapped him on the shoulder, whispering something Julia couldn't hear.

"Excuse me, Julia," Austin said. "I've got to talk to Lucas for a minute." The two guys moved away from the table. Lucas started talking quietly to Austin as if what he had to say was terribly confidential, terribly important. Julia hoped it wouldn't take too long.

Courtney spoke up again. "That dress is . . . interesting. Did you get it at a mall in New York?"

Julia took a quick sip of her soda. "No. I got it at a boutique where they sell vintage clothes."

"Vintage?" Courtney raised her eyebrows quizzically.

"You know, antique," Julia clarified. "This isn't

35

exactly antique, though. It's from the late sixties or early seventies, I think."

Courtney drew back in her chair. "You mean somebody else wore it? Somebody you don't even know?" She made a sour face.

Julia chewed a bite of her hamburger. It was tasting more and more like glue. And she was beginning to wish she could glue Courtney's mouth shut.

"Tell us about the malls in New York," Tiffany said. Amber nodded.

Julia gave a little shrug. "I've never been to a mall."

Now all three girls looked at her as if she had antennae growing out of her head. "What! No malls!"

Julia gave up on the hamburger. She couldn't eat with three people staring at her as if she were from outer space.

"It's just that there are so many places to shop in the city," she said hurriedly, her words tumbling over each other. "There are department stores like Macy's. And all kinds of little boutiques downtown—that's where my friends and I usually go. They have the coolest clothes there. You wouldn't believe the people you see!"

She went on to talk about her sightings of Ethan Hawke and Christy Turlington.

"One time I was even next to Julia Roberts in the dressing room," she said. "At least, I *think* it was Julia Roberts." She started laughing.

Her laughter died when she saw the way the three girls across the table were exchanging glances. She wasn't exactly sure what they were telegraphing

36

to each other, but she knew that it was about her and that it wasn't complimentary.

"You must feel so out of place in this little hick town, Julia," Courtney said, leaning forward on her elbows. "I've never seen a celebrity in person. Have you, Amber? Tiff?" The other two girls shook their heads, and the three of them started to giggle. Julia now felt extremely uncomfortable. She turned to look at Austin. He and Lucas were still talking quietly at the other end of the table. Gavin had moved down next to them and was sitting there nodding, his head bobbing up and down every time one of the other guys said anything. Julia abruptly got to her feet. *When the going gets tough, the tough get going,* she thought.

"Have a nice lunch, everyone," she said as she picked up her tray and walked away. She was hoping that Austin would come after her.

He didn't.

Austin had been bored by his conversation with Lucas. Or more like his lecture. Lucas had been doing all the talking while he and Gavin were virtual prisoners. All Austin had wanted was a nice, get-to-know-one-another lunch with Julia, and here she was leaving before he'd even had a chance to talk with her.

"Sit down, Austin! Let her go!" Lucas put a hand on Austin's arm. "She looks pretty steamed up. Let her cool down."

Austin hesitated for a moment, debating

whether or not to go after her, then sank back into his chair. "Why did she leave without saying good-bye?" he asked Courtney.

"Like I know," Courtney said flippantly, moving down to join them. "What was with her? 'I don't go to malls,'" she mimicked in a syrupy, singsong voice. "'I shop with movie stars and models.' She was going on and on. Didn't you hear her?"

Austin folded his arms over his chest. "No. I didn't hear her because Lucas insisted that there was something he had to tell me immediately."

He regarded Lucas with a cool stare. "What exactly was so urgent about the pep rally? And you've never cared about fighting with your father before. You can't honestly tell me that those things were too important to wait."

Lucas shrugged. He picked up an olive from the half-eaten food on Austin's plate and popped it in his mouth.

"Well," Courtney cut in, "she was rude to get up and leave like that. She didn't even say goodbye to you. You think that's rude, don't you?"

"Of course it's rude!" Lucas interjected. "Completely lacking in class."

After a moment Austin stood up, tucked his books under his arm, and grabbed his tray. "See you guys later," he mumbled.

"Hey, what's wrong?" Lucas called after him.

Austin looked back over his shoulder. "You are," he said, and kept walking.

# Four

JULIA'S PULSE WAS racing as she left the cafeteria. Her emotions tumbled in a mixture of shock and hurt at the way Austin and his friends had treated her.

As the day wore on, however, she began to wonder if she had taken things the wrong way. *What if I totally overreacted, and now Austin thinks I'm completely nuts?* she asked herself miserably. There was no doubt that Courtney had been rude to her, but Austin didn't know that. Then again, Austin shouldn't have ignored her the entire time.

For the rest of the afternoon, she carried on a running argument with herself. First she'd tell herself she'd been right to feel insulted. Then she'd decide that she had been overly sensitive. Neither side won. She felt more homesick for her friends than ever.

She sat in her last class with her eyes glued to the clock. *Come on, move those hands and let me out of here*, she urged silently.

At last the final bell rang. Julia could hardly wait to get away from Sullivan High. She raced to her locker, grabbed her coat, and ran out the double doors.

Kayla fell into step beside her as she was chugging toward the parking lot. "Are you all right?" she asked. "I saw you sitting with Austin and his friends . . . and I saw you get up and walk away. You looked pretty mad."

*Terrific*, Julia thought. *If you saw the whole scene, plenty of other people did too. Totally not the way I wanted to make a first impression at my new school.*

"I was upset," Julia told her.

"What happened?"

Julia let out a long sigh. "Courtney was dissing me. And I felt like Austin was ignoring me. But maybe I was just being oversensitive. You know, being the new girl and all."

Kayla looked thoughtful. "Maybe. But it is tough being around Austin and his friends. They're definitely a cliquish bunch. And I'll tell you something else: Courtney Kendall would have her claws out for anyone who came between her and Austin Worth."

Julia kicked at a pebble. "But Austin was the one who asked me to lunch. I'd never try to snag someone else's boyfriend."

"Boyfriend! You think Austin is Courtney's boyfriend?" Kayla wrinkled her nose. "In her

40

dreams. She's been after him for ages, but Austin is only her boyfriend *in her mind*. You've got nothing to worry about there."

A few hours earlier Julia's heart would have danced at what Kayla had just told her. Now she wasn't so sure she wanted Austin after his friends had been so rude to her.

Julia shook her head. "It doesn't matter anyway. If Austin's friends are such jerks, what does that say about him?"

"Austin's different. He's cooler than his friends. They've just all hung out forever," Kayla told her. "You can explain things to him tomorrow. He's a pretty understanding guy."

"I don't know," Julia said. "Maybe you're right. I'm totally confused."

"I understand. It must be rough to be the new girl," Kayla said as they approached Julia's car. "But if you want to learn a little about Austin Worth, you should stop by the library in town on a Tuesday after school."

Julia opened her car door and then turned back to Kayla.

"Why?"

Kayla smiled and put her hands on her hips. "Go see for yourself."

Julia filed the information in her mind. "I'll remember that." She got in her car, slid behind the wheel, and looked back at Kayla. "Thanks for listening."

"Anytime."

*       *       *

"Why the long face?" Tony asked as soon as Julia walked over to him at the garage that afternoon.

Julia sighed. "I didn't realize it was so obvious."

Tony gave her a half smile. "The only way you could be more obvious is if you wore a sign around your neck that said 'I'm miserable.' What's wrong?"

Julia shook her head. "Never mind, Tony. You barely know me. I don't want to bother you with my problems."

"I know why you won't tell me," he said, faking a pout. "You think I'm not sensitive enough. I've got news for you: I'm one of the most sensitive guys around. Sensitivity is my middle name."

Julia couldn't help smiling as she looked at Tony—a six-foot-tall, muscular mechanic who was boasting about his sensitivity.

"C'mon, tell me what's bugging you," he urged.

"Okay," Julia said after a moment. She leaned against a Ford Mustang. "I'm not exactly hitting it off with people at school."

"All the people, or just some people?"

Julia raked her fingers through her hair. "Some people. The guy who owns that car, for instance." She pointed to the black BMW that was fixed and waiting to be picked up. Ever since Max had given her the job, she'd worked on the dent almost non-stop all weekend.

Tony's eyes widened. "Lucas Malloy?"

"Yeah. I'm the one who dented his fender."

Tony slapped his forehead with his hand. "You're kidding."

"No. It wasn't my fault, though. The guy was all over the road. Then he slammed on his brakes without any warning at all. It's a miracle he ended up with only a dented fender."

Tony tapped one end of a wrench lightly in the palm of his hand. "That guy brings his car here banged up all the time. Always claims it's somebody else's fault. I believed him at first, but then it just didn't add up."

Tony paused, gathering his thoughts. "Lucas is a hothead. You shouldn't take it personally."

"I know," Julia said softly. "But then today I thought his friends were being rude to me. Maybe I was being a little too sensitive, though."

Tony tilted his head to one side. "Not to worry. You can straighten it out—you're just getting to know everybody."

Julia let out another long sigh.

"Something tells me there's more to the story," Tony said.

Julia bit her lip. "There is. I like another guy in the crowd. I mean, I *liked* him. I don't know. He's Lucas's best friend, and I think I might have messed things up with him because I didn't get along with his friends."

Tony twirled the wrench in his hands. "Well, if this guy can't make up his own mind about you, then he's not worth your time."

"You make it sound so simple."

"It's not simple," Tony said. "A best friend's opinion is always important. I'm sure you know that."

"Right," Julia said. She was surprised that she was feeling better, even though her problem wasn't resolved. Talking to Tony had helped. It felt comfortable.

She was about to say more, when Tony gave her a nudge. "Hey, speak of the devil. Look who's here, driving up in Daddy's car."

Julia turned and saw a Mercedes Benz pulling into the lot. Lucas Malloy was behind the wheel. His friend Gavin was with him.

Tony threw his rag into a bucket. "I'm going to let you handle this. After all, you fixed the car. I'll be around, though, and my dad is in the office, just in case you have a problem." He picked up the rag bucket and lugged it inside the garage.

"Is my car ready?" Lucas asked shortly as he and Gavin got out of the car.

"It's over there." Julia pointed to where the car was parked beside the garage. She felt awkward around Lucas and Gavin after what had happened at lunch.

"Let's have a look at it, then," Lucas said. He walked past Julia and bent down to examine the BMW's fender.

Julia watched as Lucas put his face inches from the fender and stared at it. He moved back, then up close again. Then he ran his hand over the spot where the dent had been fixed.

Julia tapped her foot impatiently. "Well?"

"I'm not sure," he said. He looked over his shoulder at Gavin. "Come here and check this out."

Gavin ambled over and took a look. "The job is

perfect," he said. "You couldn't see any damage if you had a microscope."

"Yeah," Lucas agreed. He stood up. "Nice job."

Julia didn't think he sounded too sincere. "Thanks," she said simply, trying to sound pleasant. "I can see why you worry about the car. It's a beauty."

Lucas nodded. Max walked up to them at that moment. "What do you think of the job, Malloy?" he asked.

"It looks good," Lucas told him.

Max beamed. "Glad you're happy. Just sign the form stating you've received the car in good condition."

Max held out a form and a pen on a clipboard. Lucas scribbled his name on the dotted line. Then he examined the bill and handed Max some cash.

"Okay, we're settled," Max said. "Good afternoon, guys."

Lucas nodded to Max and Julia. Without another word he got in his car, and Gavin walked toward the Mercedes.

Julia let out a deep breath as she watched Lucas and Gavin drive away. Lucas hadn't been outright nasty like he'd been the other day, but he'd been far from friendly. And something told her that no matter what she did, he would never like her . . . nor would she like him. Even if he was Austin Worth's best friend.

# Five

T HE FOLLOWING MORNING before homeroom, Julia scanned Sullivan High's jam-packed hallway for a sign of Austin. *I want to see him and I don't,* she thought.

Before she could think too much about it, Austin fell into step beside her. "Hi, you," he said.

Julia's heart leaped. Then a pang of doubt stabbed her. *Why didn't he make a point of apologizing to me yesterday?* "Hi," she mumbled, suddenly feeling tongue-tied.

"Oh, Austin! Austin!" A girl wiggled her fingers in a wave, trying to get his attention. Julia realized it was the girl who had asked her about her lipstick and then had dissed her. Suddenly uncomfortable, Julia hurried to her locker.

Austin nodded briefly to the girl, then hurried after Julia, dodging through the crowd. "Wait up!" he called.

Julia kept walking. She saw the questioning looks as she passed. Everyone was wondering how this new girl got one of the hottest guys in school to run after her. Julia could feel their eyes on her; she could sense the way they were checking out her clothes. She told herself to blow it off.

Julia reached her locker and dropped her books in front of it. She started spinning the dial of her lock, clicking off the combination.

"Look, Julia," Austin said to her back, "I know you got angry at lunch yesterday. But I wish you hadn't left without saying anything to me."

Julia turned around. She still felt confused about what had happened at lunch, but as she stared once again into Austin's gorgeous eyes, all she could think about was how attracted she was to him. "I guess I flew off the handle," she said slowly. "I shouldn't have stormed out of the cafeteria like that."

Austin shrugged. "I'm sure you had your reasons. I know that Courtney isn't always the friendliest person. And Lucas was talking my ear off—I should have stopped him." He put his hands on her shoulders and leaned in close. Julia felt weak from the warmth of his touch. "Let me make it up to you," he said. "Would you go out with me tomorrow night?"

"Tomorrow?" she repeated dumbly, unable to find the words to say anything more.

"I mean no disrespect, ma'am," Austin told her, faking a southern drawl. "I know it's short notice. It's just that I'd like to take you to the pep rally."

47

Julia wrinkled up her nose. "Pep rally?" she echoed. Excited as she was, she couldn't disguise the skepticism in her voice.

Austin took a step back, a smile spreading across his face, making him look incredibly sexy. "I understand—it's not a sophisticated New York City thing. Just give it a try."

Julia fiddled with her backpack. "I didn't mean to put it down, it's just that I've never been to anything like that."

"I think you'll have a good time. Everybody gets revved up. They'll be a couple of bands, plus our very own marching one. What do you say? Artists are supposed to be adventurous, aren't they? Will you go?"

*Yes.* The word had already formed itself in Julia's mind. *Yes, yes, yes, yes. Why can't I just say it?* Julia asked herself. The word just wouldn't come out. *It's just a pep rally, Julia. Not a lifelong commitment.*

She found herself tapping her foot and trying to look vaguely disinterested. "Well . . . I'm not sure. I'll be working at Max's Garage tomorrow, so maybe I'll just, like, show up if I can."

"Yeah, well, I hope you can make it." Austin squeezed her shoulder before he walked away. After feeling the goose bumps spread through her body at his touch, Julia couldn't help smiling.

She was still walking on air when she entered homeroom. Kayla looked at her questioningly. "What's that look on your face, Julia? You look like you died and went to heaven."

Julia sat down and rubbed at a spot on her desk. "Austin asked me out—to the pep rally tomorrow night." Julia laughed to herself as she realized that she sounded like the stereotypical lovesick teenager that she used to make fun of—but that's how she felt.

Kayla's eyes grew wide. "Fast work! You're going to have a great time."

"Well . . . I don't know. . . ."

"Huh? What do you mean you don't know?" Kayla demanded. "You said yes, didn't you? Julia, Austin Worth is just about the nicest, hottest guy in school. Tell me you said yes."

Julia gave her head a little shake. "Well, I didn't say no." She clicked her tongue against her teeth. "It's just that his whole crowd is so different from me. They act like I don't belong—"

"Forget it!" Kayla cut her off. "You've got more guts than to let them get to you. Don't worry about them; worry about him, and everything will take care of itself. Things will work out fine."

Mrs. Johnston, her homeroom teacher, began the school announcements, but Julia was so wrapped up in her own thoughts that she didn't hear a word. *I only wish everything would be as easy as you say, Kayla.*

But Julia was still on cloud nine about Austin as she went to her first class. It was English, which she had missed yesterday because of her tour with Kayla. Julia handed her registration card to the teacher, a wiry, redheaded man named Mr. Rathbone who wore a red bow tie. Julia thought he looked a little like Woody Allen.

"Do take a seat quickly," Mr. Rathbone said. His voice was startling—high and a little squeaky. He motioned toward a desk.

At that moment, Julia came crashing back to earth: The only vacant seat in the room was between Courtney and Lucas.

*I can't get away from these two.*

They both smiled at her as she sat down, but their smiles looked stiff and fake. Julia could feel a chill in the air as she took a pen out of her backpack.

Out of the corner of her eye, she saw Courtney look her up and down, then lean across the aisle and whisper something to her girlfriend. The girl, who had long, perfectly straight hair that fell to her shoulders, put her hand over her mouth to suppress a giggle. Courtney whispered again. More giggles. Julia glanced at Lucas and saw him watching the two of them with a smirk on his face.

Julia pretended she didn't notice. She kept her eyes straight ahead and gritted her teeth. *I will not, will not, let you embarrass me,* she told them silently.

She took a deep breath. She'd follow Kayla's advice about Austin's friends: *"Don't worry about them; worry about him."*

The rest of the day Julia kept noticing Austin watching her. They didn't have any classes together, and they didn't sit together at lunch, but they stole glances at each other—across the hallway, in the stairwell, in the cafeteria. They carried on a silent flirtation with their eyes.

Since she didn't have work after school that day, Julia decided to check out Local Color, the only art store in town. She needed to get some turpentine to replace the can that she had somehow misplaced during the move.

Instead of turning down Main Street, where the art store was located, however, she changed her mind and drove toward the library on Monagle Street. A teacher at Crate had suggested she look at the work of printmaker Giorgio Morandi. The faculty at Crate were always going out of their way to recommend points of interest to the students. Julia missed that.

*Okay, so it was a year ago when that teacher mentioned Morandi,* Julia admitted as she pulled into a parking space. *Maybe a local branch library isn't too likely to have anything on him, but I might as well take a look.*

As she headed up the walk to the library, Julia pulled the collar of her authentic World War II leather flight jacket close around her throat. Indian summer was gone for good. The crisp chill in the air made Julia think of raking leaves, toasting marshmallows, and drinking hot cider. The type of thing she'd fantasized about as a city kid. Naturally, she didn't picture herself alone in those daydreams. Austin Worth was there with her.

Julia pushed open the door to the library and was charmed by what she saw. The checkout desk was right in the center, and it divided the interior

51

into two rooms, one for children and one for adults. The latter was filled with chintz-covered sofas, and its walls were covered with Norman Rockwell prints. It looked very cozy and quaint.

Julia walked over to the desk. "I'm looking for a book on Giorgio Morandi," she told the tiny librarian whose name tag said "Mildred Gilhooley." "Morandi is an artist—"

Mildred Gilhooley cut her off. "Oh, dear, you don't have to tell *me*. Morandi is one of my favorites." Her eyes crinkled at the corners as she smiled. She insisted on getting the books for Julia and even steered her to a comfortable chair.

Julia scanned the room as she sat back in the chair. "Do you need something else, dear?" Mildred asked.

"Oh, um, no. I'm fine," Julia replied. She was thumbing through the first book Mildred had given her when the sight of a redheaded toddler lugging a large picture book caught her eye. The book was almost bigger than he was, and he kept stumbling and dropping the book. Still, when his mother tried to take it from him, he shook his head vigorously and clung to the book harder than ever. A few steps behind the boy, a little girl with dark curly hair carried a book of her own. She was followed by an Asian boy in denim overalls. More children followed in a line into the children's room.

Julia put down her book and walked over to the librarian. "What's going on?" she asked, gesturing toward the line of kids.

"Story hour," the librarian whispered. "Every Tuesday. We have the most wonderful young man who reads stories to the kids. He volunteers. Such a handsome young man too."

"Oh." Julia felt her pulse quicken. Could it be? She put her book down on her chair and tried to appear casual as she strolled toward the children's room.

About fifteen little kids, some with their mothers or fathers, were seated on the floor staring at Austin. He was reading a story about a kitten who needed a home. Every so often he would hold up the book and say something about the picture while the kids oohed and aaahed. Julia's heart swelled in her chest. Not only was Austin sexy, he was also sensitive enough to volunteer to read to toddlers. *Face it, Julia. He's about as perfect as can be.*

Austin held up a picture and suddenly saw Julia standing there. Their eyes locked.

"Read the story! Read the story!" a toddler piped up. Soon the rest of the kids joined in.

Julia raised her hand gently and whispered, "Good-bye."

Austin smiled and nodded back.

As Julia turned to go, she felt a glow of warmth run through her entire body. She pushed open the library door and hurried outside.

"You forgot your books!" Mildred called after her.

"That's okay," she called back as she headed to her car. "I didn't really come for the books anyway," she added in a whisper.

# Six

"YOU'RE LOOKING VERY corporate, Mom," Julia teased as she walked into the kitchen and saw her mother eating breakfast. Ann Marin was dressed in a navy wool skirt and matching blazer.

"That's the idea, dear," her mother replied. "I kind of miss the days when I could go to work in jeans, but I make a lot more money now than I did keeping the books for a few stores. This is the way everyone dresses at the office. As they say, when in Rome . . ."

"Do as the Romans do," Julia finished for her. "I don't dress like the other kids at school."

"That's not quite the same thing."

Julia poured herself a bowl of cornflakes and a cup of coffee and sat down next to her mother. "Have you seen Gizmo? That cat has been hiding most of the time since we got here. I guess he's freaked out about moving."

Mrs. Marin shrugged. "I saw him prowling around on the porch last night, and his food dish was empty this morning. Give him time, he'll adjust." She took a bite of toast and regarded her daughter thoughtfully. "You look awfully happy. Did you find out school is better than you thought?"

"No, not at all." Julia smiled and took a sip of her coffee. "Just kidding. I guess it's not *so* bad. Actually, I met a guy. I have a date tonight."

"A date? Tonight?" Her mother raised her eyebrows. "Who is he?"

Julia quickly filled her mother in on meeting Austin, including the run-in with Lucas and how she ended up fixing his car.

"If you fixed the guy's car, that ought to have changed his mind."

"Not really."

"Well, don't worry about it. Just go out with Austin and let him deal with his friends. I'm sure once they get to know you, they'll like you."

*Fat chance,* Julia thought. But to her mother she simply said, "We'll see."

"Right. Oh, by the way," her mother said, "I got your schedule mixed up yesterday, and I stopped by the garage to see you. I met Max. He's a nice guy."

"Yeah, he's all right," Julia agreed.

"Mmm." Her mother took a quick sip of her coffee. "I've got to go, I'll be late for work," she said quickly. She grabbed her briefcase and was out the door.

For a split second Julia thought she'd detected a flush on her mother's pale cheeks. A flush that had nothing to do with being late for work.

Austin leaned against Julia's locker and crossed one foot over the other. He watched Lucas Malloy maneuver his 200-pound frame through Sullivan's crowded halls before homeroom, checking out the girls, nodding hellos, and giving high fives to the guys.

A smile flickered across Austin's face. He always got a kick out of the way Lucas loved to play the big-man-on-campus role. "Hey, bud," he called to him.

Lucas cut through the crowd. "Hey." He stood next to Austin. "What's the deal? Your home-room's in the other direction."

Austin faked a double take. "No way, really?" he teased. "No, seriously, I'm just waiting for somebody."

"This is that girl's locker, isn't it?"

Austin took a deep breath. "Her name's Julia, Lucas."

"Austin, buddy, we've been over this already. You're taking this too fast."

"Don't worry about it. I know what I'm doing. I thought I'd take her to the pep rally and maybe show her around a little."

Lucas's jaw dropped. "You're taking her on a *date?* You can't do that!"

"I don't think I heard you right. Are you telling me what to do?"

Lucas's eyes shifted from left to right. "No. Yes.

I don't know. Look, man, I'm your best friend. I'm trying to save you from yourself. If you take her to that pep rally, you'll look like a fool."

"Stop making such a big deal out of this," Austin said, tired of arguing. "It's just . . ." He sighed. "It's just the decent thing to do. I want to make a new student feel at home, that's all."

Lucas leaned against the locker. "Since when did you become a one-man welcome committee?" Then he dropped his voice to a whisper. "Listen, walk with me, okay? I've got to tell you something."

Austin's eyes narrowed. "Why so mysterious?"

"Because I don't want to make a big announcement. Trust me, this is important," Lucas insisted.

Austin scanned the hallway for a sign of Julia. There was none. "Okay, okay, tell me the big secret."

Lucas walked him a few paces down the hall. "Remember when she fixed my car?" he asked in a hushed voice.

"Of course. She did a great job too."

"Yeah, well, okay, she did," Lucas said grudgingly. "But that's not the point."

"Then get to the point. I wish you'd stop whispering!" Austin said with an edge of exasperation in his voice.

"When I dropped off the car at Max's, I'd left my mother's birthday present in the glove compartment. It was a set of crystal candlesticks. When I picked up the car, they were gone."

Austin's eyebrows shot up. "What are you saying?

That she stole them? What would Julia want with crystal candlesticks?"

Lucas looked at Austin as if he'd asked an incredibly dense question. "They're worth a lot of money," he said, putting emphasis on each word.

Austin blinked a few times. "Did you ask Max about them?"

Lucas nodded. "Sure. He hadn't seen them. And if I ask Julia, I'm sure she'd just deny it."

"I can't believe that she would steal those candlesticks. Maybe you misplaced them or left them somewhere."

Lucas looked thoughtful. "Maybe. I know this whole thing sounds wild." Lucas paused, running a hand through his hair. "You know what? I know some people in New York City, and I think I'm going to ask around about her."

Austin gave a low chuckle. "Oh, right. There are about eight million people in New York City. You think someone you know will just happen to know Julia?"

"It's not so far-fetched. We're only talking about people in high school. We know she went to that High School of Creative Arts. All I have to do is ask around and find someone who either goes there or knows someone who does."

Austin shook his head. "If you ask me, you're being kind of strange, acting so suspicious and talking about playing detective. It's just not your style, Lucas."

"Well, it's my style when my best friend is concerned. We're always number one with each other, right? Numero uno?"

Austin didn't say anything for a moment.

"Right?" Lucas prompted.

"Yes," Austin responded in a low voice.

"I'm only trying to look out for you, Austin."

Austin nodded. He spotted Julia coming down the hall and started heading toward her. "I'll catch you later, Lucas."

"Don't forget what I told you," Lucas called after him.

Austin looked over his shoulder. "I won't. But you're wrong."

But as Austin approached Julia, he wondered how sure he could be that Lucas was wrong. *What did happen to those candlesticks?*

"Hi there," Austin greeted Julia when he reached her.

She smiled brightly. "Hi, yourself." Austin studied her face. He had forgotten how beautiful she was. He opened his mouth to ask about the candlesticks, but no words came out. "Is something the matter, Austin?" Julia asked.

He shook his head. "No. How's the job at the garage?" he blurted out. *Smooth, Austin, very smooth.*

Julia looked at him questioningly. "It's going great. What made you ask?"

Austin shrugged. "Just wondering, that's all."

He looked into Julia's eyes—the eyes that made his heart do a little flip. "Are you going to make it to the pep rally?"

"Definitely," she said.

He was now completely torn between his loyalty to Lucas and his attraction to Julia. He didn't know what to say. "Cool. I'll be taking pictures for the paper, so look for the guy running around with a camera. See you there." His words felt unnatural as he heard them aloud.

Austin turned away abruptly. As he headed down the hall, he could feel Julia's eyes staring at his back.

Julia didn't see Austin for the rest of the day. He didn't sit at his usual table with the rest of his crowd at lunch. She didn't even run into him in the halls.

"I just don't get it," she told Kayla as she got her books out of her locker after last period. "When he made the date with me for the pep rally, it was kind of short notice . . . but he acted so interested. Then this morning he was so weird—jumpy and kind of distant."

"It probably had nothing to do with you," Kayla insisted. "Put it out of your mind until you see him tonight. Take it from there." Julia tried to take Kayla's advice. She went to work and pumped gas, cleaned windshields, and changed tires. She kidded around with Tony and made conversation with Max. But her thoughts kept returning to Austin. After what seemed like an eternity, it was time to close up. Julia grabbed the jeans and sweater she'd brought to change into and headed for the ladies' room. There she removed her mechanic's overalls and washed her hands carefully in the sink. She tied back her hair and washed her face. Then she took out her makeup case and applied just a little—mascara and lip gloss. She brushed out her hair and decided to wear it down.

Julia liked what she saw in the mirror. The black sweater with the zippers up the arms was pretty warm, so she'd only needed her lightweight, form-fitting jacket that set off her narrow waist.

Julia applied a second coat of mascara, then decided to use a bit of blush. Then she put her hair back up. No, that didn't look right. She let her hair down again. Then she dabbed some honeysuckle perfume on her wrists. *No use stalling,* she told herself. *Go to the pep rally and face the music.* She took one last look in the mirror and went out to meet Tony, who was dropping her off.

When Julia arrived at the football field, the pep rally was well under way and the bleachers were packed.

It was like nothing she'd seen at Crate. "This is kind of cool," she admitted, taking everything in.

The band was blasting out a rousing march while members of the drill team pirouetted around them. In front of the bleachers, the cheerleaders shot into the air in whirls and tumbles, whipping the crowd into such a frenzy that the stands were practically rocking. The air crackled with excitement.

Julia searched for Austin, her eyes sweeping in every direction. *How will I ever find him in this crowd?* She kicked up a little cloud of dirt, trying to look nonchalant as she stood watching the marching band. Then in an instant everything came to a halt. The band major blew a whistle three times, and all activity and noise stopped. The band fell silent, and the cheerleaders and drill team stood motionless with their pom-poms on their hips.

The announcement boomed over the loudspeaker: "Introducing the players of this season's Sullivan High Varsity Football Team!"

The bleachers erupted with a frenzy of cheering. *"Hurrraayy!"*

Players began trotting out under the goalpost. The crowd was roaring, making it easy for Julia to get caught up in the excitement, in the energy and color and the rush of music. If only she could find Austin.

She decided to make a quick trip to the concession stand, although she knew she couldn't eat a thing. At least it would give her something to do. She was so nervous, her stomach was doing more back flips than the cheerleaders. While she was waiting in line, she felt a tap on her shoulder. She whirled around and looked right up into Austin's face.

"Hey, I've been looking all over for you," he said.

"Well, here I am," Julia replied, gazing at him with a smile. She liked what she saw. His face was ruddy from the crisp air and his eyes were sparkling. She studied the thirty-five-millimeter camera that hung on a strap around his neck. "That must have set you back some bucks," she commented. "I'd love to have a camera like that; I was going to take photography this year. I love black-and-white portraits."

"So do I. But for sports action shots I really need color."

Julia nodded in agreement. "It brings out the energy and the movement."

"I've been meaning to ask you if you wanted to do some work for the paper. We could use some fresh ideas, and with all your art training, I bet you'd be great."

Julia hesitated. "I'm pretty busy with school and my job."

"Well, think about it. Anyway, I've got to take a couple more shots. I'll just be a few minutes."

"Sure," Julia said. She watched as Austin ran back toward the football field. She couldn't take her eyes off him as he took shot after shot, shuffling about to get the team from a variety of angles, moving in close and pulling back, sometimes dropping down on one knee.

Julia thought about what she'd just told Austin. And it was true. She *did* wish she had a camera just like his. Because if she did, she'd take a whole roll of shots of beautiful Austin Worth.

# Seven

THE FOOTBALL PLAYERS had retreated into the locker room, and the crowd in the bleachers was beginning to thin out. Austin was making his way across the football field. As he approached, Julia suddenly had this wild fantasy that he would sweep her into his arms. The idea made her heart pound faster.

No such thing happened. "I think I got a lot of good shots," Austin said as he stepped up next to her. He replaced the lens cap on his camera.

A gust of wind ruffled his soft dark hair. Julia resisted the impulse to run her fingers through it. "I really am having a good time," Julia said. "I guess I didn't know what to expect. We didn't have things like this at my old school." She laughed. "We didn't even have a football team."

Austin nodded and folded his arms. He regarded her steadily, as if he was turning over thoughts in his mind.

After a few moments of silence, Julia began to fidget. "Is there something wrong?" she asked.

"Pardon me for staring," Austin apologized, still keeping his eyes intensely on her. "It's just that you're different, and I like that. I like listening to you. I like looking at you."

*You're pretty sure of yourself,* Julia thought as she watched Austin calmly stand there. It sent a prickle of irritation up her spine that he could get to her so easily.

But Julia didn't have time to say anything. Lucas appeared out of nowhere and gave Austin a hefty pat on the back, sending Austin tumbling forward. "Hey, pal!" he bellowed. Lucas carried his football helmet in one hand and a water bottle in the other. Courtney, Tiffany, and Gavin were with him.

"Well, well, well, what have we here?" Lucas opened his eyes wide and looked Julia up and down. He turned to Courtney and the others to include them. "I would have thought a pep rally wouldn't be quite sophisticated enough for someone who shops with movie stars every day," he said with the barest trace of a smirk. The others chuckled.

"Come on, Lucas," Austin cautioned.

"I was only fooling around," Lucas said. "Julia knows that, don't you, Julia?"

There was a moment of uncomfortable silence. "Sure," Julia said thinly. What would be the point in starting an argument with Lucas?

"All right!" Lucas pumped his water bottle in the

air. He slapped Austin on the shoulder. "See you later, buddy." He trotted off, and the others followed.

"What a jerk," Julia blurted out angrily. The words were out of her mouth before she even realized she'd said them.

Austin's expression stiffened. "Lucas is my best friend," he stated coldly. He looked at the ground for a moment, then back up at Julia.

Julia didn't respond. Even if she had been wrong to say it aloud, Lucas *was* a jerk. There was no denying it.

"But I will admit that he acted pretty stupid just now." Austin's voice was friendly again. "He shouldn't have made that remark. That's Lucas for you, always trying to be a comedian." He put his hands on Julia's shoulders. The gesture made Julia's knees feel a little shaky. "Are we okay now?" he asked.

Julia nodded. "It wasn't you I was angry with."

Austin dropped his hands, stuffing them into his pockets. He smiled mischievously. "Well, you may not believe it, but years ago I was a scrawny kid. Bigger kids used to pick on me all the time. Lucas put a stop to it. He was always big, and he used to beat them up and scare them off for me."

"So that's why you two became friends."

"Yeah. He's always been there for me. Anyway, why am I talking about Lucas? I want to talk about you." He looked into her eyes. "I hardly know where to start."

She looked up at him. "Actually, there's something I've been wanting to ask *you*."

"Ask away," he said. Austin took her hand in his,

and his touch made her heart flutter lightly. They started walking toward the football field.

"That children's story group at the library," Julia began. "It's such an usual thing for a guy to do. Why do you do it?"

Austin looked away and didn't answer for a moment. "It looks good on college applications," he finally responded.

Julia knitted her brows. "That's why?"

"Yeah." Austin nodded. "You know how competitive it is."

"I guess," Julia said. Maybe Austin wasn't as sensitive as she'd thought.

"Anyway, tell me what it's like in New York," Austin asked, swinging their arms back and forth.

"Oh, I love it there," Julia's voice swelled with emotion. "Of course, our apartment was too small and the ceiling leaked when it rained. I had to do my painting in a corner of my bedroom, so it always smelled like turpentine."

"I can see why you loved it," Austin joked.

Julia laughed. "Let me finish," she said, poking him playfully in the ribs. "The great thing about New York is that there are so many places to go and things to see. You could live there all your life and keep discovering things."

"Like . . . ?" Austin prompted.

"Like the different neighborhoods. Itxey—she's my best friend—Itxey and I would always go exploring. I was sixteen before I knew there was a Chinatown in Brooklyn, not just in Manhattan. It was Itxey who showed it to me. We spent a lot of time in museums too. One time, the two of us sat in front of a Vincent van Gogh painting for an entire afternoon."

"You must miss her," Austin said. He stopped walking for a moment. "Anyone else you miss? A guy, maybe?"

Julia thought of Zeke. It seemed as if they had been together a hundred years ago. "Not really," she answered slowly. "Things between my boyfriend and me were kind of over before I left. I liked him, but it was never anything serious."

"Good," Austin said simply. He squeezed her hand gently, then laced his fingers through hers. They resumed walking and didn't say anything more. It was cold out, but Julia felt warm.

They reached the end of the football field, then started back toward the parking lot. Austin dropped her hand and put his arm around her. Julia leaned against him, feeling a little light-headed. They seemed to fit together perfectly.

"Let's take a ride over to Hot Rods," Austin suggested. "It's a new place downtown. Everyone's going after the rally." He stopped walking and stepped in front of her. "I know you'll get along great with everyone once you all get to know each other."

Julia felt herself falling from the clouds and plummeting back to earth. *No, no, no. Being around "everyone" will ruin everything.*

But Austin was smiling down at her, looking into her eyes expectantly, waiting for her answer.

She couldn't think of a good reason to say no without sounding silly.

"All right," she heard herself say reluctantly. "Let's go to Hot Rods."

Hot Rods was nothing like the dark little hole-in-the-wall East Village places in which Julia used to hang out in New York. It was brightly colored and decorated like a glorified old-fashioned 1950s diner. The walls were covered with paintings of 1950s cars, and a huge red hot rod stood in the middle of the floor.

Austin led Julia to a booth. In a moment a waitress wearing roller skates wheeled up to take their order.

"I'll have a burger and a chocolate shake," Austin told the waitress.

"Just coffee for me," Julia ordered. She looked around the restaurant, relieved that none of Austin's friends had arrived.

Austin reached across the table and took her hand. "Take it easy," he said. "You look like you're about to jump out of your skin."

"I'm okay . . . really."

"My friends aren't that terrible," he told her soothingly. "You guys just got started off on the wrong foot, that's all."

Julia gently withdrew her hand from his. "It isn't just your friends . . . it's everything. Everything is so different here." She looked into Austin's eyes. "Everything is happening so fast."

Austin rested his hand lightly on hers. "I think I know what you mean. I feel it too."

"You do?" Julia whispered.

"Since the first moment I saw you." Austin got up and sat beside Julia in the booth, so close that their bodies were touching from hip to knee. "Relax." He kissed her forehead, his lips brushing her skin lightly and quickly.

Julia opened her mouth to speak, but before she could say anything, Lucas walked into the restaurant, his arm around Tiffany. Courtney and a few others followed.

Lucas spotted Austin and Julia immediately, giving them a big wave. Julia felt her heart sink as Lucas led the crowd toward their table.

Julia suddenly thought of places she'd rather be: at the garage, on a plane going to Florida, washing dishes, painting, cleaning the oven—almost anywhere.

Lucas pulled a chair out from another table, flipped it around, and sat down. He leaned his arms over the back of the chair as Tiffany, Gavin, and Courtney squeezed into the other side of the booth. "You two look cozy," Lucas said, signaling to the waitress. "Here's to the next, and last, football season at Sullivan High." He picked up a glass of water and did a mock toast. Then he looked at Julia and smiled. "And here's to Julia, the new girl at school. Did you enjoy yourself at the rally, Julia?"

Julia regarded Lucas, caught off guard that he was addressing her with a civil question. Usually he made such a point of ignoring her. *Might as well try to make peace with the guy,* she thought. "Yes," she told him, "I had a really good time. It was fun."

Lucas nodded. "Good," he said. "Hopefully, it will be the first of many good times for you."

Julia gave him a small smile. She wasn't sure how sincere he was, but at least Lucas was making an effort to get along with her.

The waitress skated up to their table with Austin's food and Julia's coffee.

Austin squeezed Julia's knee under the table as his friends placed their orders. "I'm so glad you're here," he whispered, his breath hot in her ear.

"Me too," she whispered back.

"So," Tiffany addressed Julia, pulling her out of her blissful moment with Austin. "How do you like Sullivan High so far?"

"I don't know," Julia answered, pouring some milk into her coffee. "It's too soon to tell. Sullivan's definitely different from my old school." She took a sip of coffee. "But I guess different can be both good and bad."

Lucas grabbed a french fry off Austin's plate. "How open-minded of you," he joked. Julia looked down at her coffee cup. She didn't like the teasing tone in Lucas's voice.

*Chill out,* she instructed herself a second later. *Don't be oversensitive.*

The waitress came back with more food. "Guess what, Julia?" Courtney said brightly, playing with the straw in the Coke in front of her. "It turns out your mother works in my mother's department. Your mom's a bookkeeper, right?"

Julia nodded. She felt her body stiffen.

Courtney smiled broadly. "My mother is your

mother's boss! Your mom is *my* mom's employee! Isn't that cute?"

Julia felt the blood drain out of her face as she stared at Courtney. Was this girl for real? Austin threw his napkin on the table. "Honestly, Courtney," he said with an edge of exasperation in his voice.

Courtney looked hurt. She stuck her lower lip out in a pout. "I was only trying to make conversation."

Julia turned to Austin. "Are you ready to go?" she asked him. "I'm a little tired."

Austin pushed his plate away. "Yeah, let's call it a night."

Julia stood up. "'Bye, everyone," she said stiffly.

"Hey, don't leave. Hang out," Lucas said.

Austin gave Courtney a cold look. "No, I think we had enough." He took Julia's hand. "'Bye, guys."

"I was only stating a fact," Julia heard Courtney whine after them.

Julia and Austin rode away in silence. Julia kept looking over at him. Why wasn't he saying anything?

Finally, when they had nearly reached her house, Julia spoke up. "What's the deal with your friends? Why are they so rude?"

Austin pulled his car to a stop in front of Julia's house. "Look, I'm sorry. Courtney says stupid things sometimes. But she's harmless." He let out a long sigh. "So what if your mom works for her mom? It's really not a big deal. Forget about it."

Julia's heart hammered. The truth was, no matter how much she hated to admit it, she didn't want to forget *all* of tonight—only part of it. She didn't want to forget about her time alone with Austin. His friends were jerks, but she couldn't help how she felt about him.

Austin reached over and put his hand on hers. She looked into his wonderful brown eyes, and her anger was instantly history.

Julia savored the delicious anticipation. Soon he would reach for her and slide his arms around her to pull her close. She could feel her heart thudding in her chest. He was going to kiss her. She closed her eyes.

*"Yeeeooooow!"* A horrible screech tore through the air. Austin and Julia both jumped.

A dark mass of fur with two glowing eyes suddenly landed on the hood of Austin's car, then jumped right off again.

"Gizmo!" Julia shrieked. Austin's face was white from shock. It made Julia giggle nervously. "That was my cat," Julia explained breathlessly. "Ever since we moved, he's been acting weird—nervous, spooky." Lights went on in the windows of Julia's house. She glanced up on the porch; the door was slowly opening. Her mother would be outside in a second. An audience was the last thing Julia needed for her first kiss with Austin.

"Thanks for a nice time. I should go," she said, motioning toward her house. "See you tomorrow." She opened the door and jumped out of the car before Austin had the chance to say a word.

There would be plenty of opportunities for kissing Austin. And Julia was pretty sure the wait would be worth it.

# Eight

$J$ULIA AND AUSTIN *were walking along the beach, hand in hand. The sun was going down, sinking into the ocean and sending brilliant streams of pink and orange shooting across the sky and the water. Diamonds of light sparkled on the waves. Austin turned to Julia and embraced her. She melted into his arms. In a moment his mouth was against hers, and she was swept into a passionate kiss. . . .*

"Ow!" Julia bolted up in bed as the cat landed on her chest. Two huge green eyes, set in a gray furry face, stared into her startled ones. Gizmo patted her nose with his paw.

"Drat the cat," Julia muttered. "Gizmo," she chided softly, "you just woke me from the absolutely, without a doubt, best dream I've ever had in my life." She scratched his ears. "And not only that, you interrupted what was potentially a *big* moment last night." Julia started to close her eyes to savor a few more dreamy moments. Then she noticed the time on the clock. "Aaagggh! Ten-fifteen!" She leaped out of bed and started grabbing socks and underwear. "How could I have overslept like that?"

*You know how it happened,* she told herself. *You shouldn't have started painting last night.*

It was just that her date with Austin had left her too wired to sleep. As soon as her mother went back to bed, Julia had gone into the studio and set up her easel with a fresh canvas. The painting that she had created was an abstract picture of her romantic feelings, all pastels in tender swirls of color. Before she knew it, hours had flown by.

*You should have known better,* she wailed inwardly as she raced to the bathroom.

Julia washed her face and brushed her teeth, then dashed back into the bedroom and raked a brush through her tangled mop of hair. Time was ticking by. She pulled on her ripped jeans and a bright yellow velour shirt that was laying on the floor, laced up her workboots, grabbed her book bag, and ran out the door.

By the time Julia arrived at school, it was time for gym.

"Iannicone!"

"Kazeroid!"

"Kendall!"

"Jagodinsky!"

The *clomp, clomp, clomp* of Julia's workboots

75

echoed on the polished floor as she entered the gym. Lines of girls dressed alike in ugly navy gym shorts and short-sleeved shirts were assembled for roll call. Their eyes followed Julia as she hurried to the locker room.

Julia groaned as she pulled on gym clothes and laced up her sneakers. She caught sight of her reflection in the mirror and sighed. Sullivan High's phys ed department managed to find shorts that made her look like a candidate for a fat farm.

It wasn't that gym class itself was so bad. No, Julia liked letting off steam. It was just a royal pain to have to get dressed and undressed and take a shower with a bunch of other girls—snobby ones at that—in the middle of the school day.

At Crate nobody would dream of venturing into the ancient, gross tiled locker area. At Sullivan, where the gym was state-of-the-art, showers were the rule.

But without a doubt, the worst thing about gym was that Courtney Kendall was in Julia's class. After last night, Courtney was the last person that Julia felt like seeing.

Most of the girls in class were standing around shifting from foot to foot. A couple were standing apart from the large group behind Courtney. Another little group stood behind Tiffany.

"We're choosing sides for volleyball," Ms. Leeds explained as Julia joined the group. "Courtney and Tiffany are the team captains."

*Great,* Julia thought as she took her place in the

crowd of girls that milled around like cows in a stockyard. *Maybe I'll be the last cow chosen for slaughter.*

As Julia walked by the team captains, Courtney elbowed Tiffany and whispered something behind her hand. The two girls giggled.

"Ms. Kendall, Ms. Gonzalez, is there something you would like to share with the rest of the group?" Ms. Leeds asked in a no-nonsense tone, peering over her glasses.

"No, Ms. Leeds." Courtney was barely able to get the words out before she and Tiffany doubled over with laughter.

Ms. Leeds rolled her eyes. "We don't have time for giggling!" she barked. "Settle down." She drew a vertical line in the air with her arm. "Everyone on this side is on Kendall's team. Everyone over here goes with Gonzalez."

The girls divided into groups on either side of the net. Julia was somewhat relieved to find herself on Tiffany's team. At least she had gotten stuck with the lesser of two evils. Ms. Leeds blew on the whistle that was hanging around her neck. "Let's play volleyball! Gonzalez, you have the first serve." Tiffany nodded. She held the ball in her left palm and punched it with her right fist. *Thwonk!* The ball shot over the net.

Julia had to admit that she wasn't half bad when it came to volleyball. Back at Crate, where the gym teachers didn't seem to actually be too interested in sports, volleyball and relay races comprised 90 percent of gym activity.

"Get it, Marin!" a girl behind her yelled, and Julia spiked the ball over the net. Then, a moment later, she fell to her knees to save a ball from landing just inside the boundary line and sent it rocketing over the net, winning the point and putting her team in the lead.

Soon the other girls on her team were setting her up—sending the ball her way so she could aim it where it would do the most damage. Before long her side was leading by several points.

Courtney was fuming. "What's wrong with you guys!" she yelled at her teammates. "You're not paying attention. Let's get moving!"

Courtney's team rallied and scored two points in quick succession. Then it was Julia's turn to serve. Instead of holding the ball in her palm, Julia tossed it in the air. She sprung up and slammed it so hard that it landed on the ground on the other side of the net before anyone on Courtney's team made a move. It was a perfect ace.

"Way to go, Julia!" Tiffany cheered.

Julia continued with her powerhouse serves. The other team had never seen anything like them and was totally unprepared for her. Courtney got madder and madder and yelled more and more until Ms. Leeds cautioned her about her sportsmanship.

And Courtney's complaints didn't do any good; if anything, they just aggravated her teammates. Julia's team won by ten points.

As the girls headed toward the locker room, Julia felt a pleasant, self-satisfied glow. She sat down on a bench in the locker room, pulled off her T-shirt, shorts, and socks, and tossed them into her gym bag. Then she threw her sneakers into the locker.

"Great game, Julia."

"Some serve, Marin."

"Everybody play like that where you come from?"

"Thanks, guys." Julia smiled. "Actually, volleyball was practically the only thing we ever did in gym. There wasn't any other equipment." She laughed. The girls around her laughed with her. A few of them suggested she join the volleyball team.

Julia enjoyed the feeling of being part of the community rather than an outsider. *There are some nice people at Sullivan, after all,* she thought. Grabbing a towel and some bath gel, she joined the line of girls headed for the steaming spray of the showers.

The needles of hot, then cold water refreshed her. She toweled off, got dressed, and went over to the bathroom mirror to comb out her hair. As she walked back to her locker to put on her shoes, she tensed. Her name had just been mentioned. The voice came from the other side of the lockers.

"Apparently, Julia has a reputation," the voice said.

Julia recognized the voice as Courtney's. Anger surged through her.

"What do you mean?" Julia heard Tiffany ask.

"You know, she's not exactly discriminating

about who she goes out with . . . or what she does with who she goes out with," Courtney said lightly.

Julia slammed her locker door. *Who does this witch think she is? What on earth is she talking about?*

Without thinking, she grabbed her bag and stomped around to the other side of the lockers. She was beyond furious; she couldn't believe that someone was capable of being so nasty.

Most of the other girls had cleared out of the locker room. Courtney and Tiffany were getting ready to leave, Courtney babbling about the new shoes that she wanted to buy.

"Oh, Julia, hi," Tiffany said, looking startled.

"Hello, Tiffany," Julia responded, trying to remain calm. She glared at Courtney without saying anything for a few moments.

Courtney avoided Julia's stare, shuffling aimlessly through her gym bag.

"Courtney," Julia said. She could tell that she wasn't really looking for anything.

Courtney looked at Julia expectantly, the hint of a smile curling her lips.

*Don't lose your temper, keep control,* Julia told herself.

"I heard everything that you just said about my 'reputation,'" Julia stated firmly. "I'm not even going to justify your ridiculous comments by defending myself. You're not worth my time."

Tiffany had gone pale.

Courtney began to fuss with her hair. "Julia, I think you—"

"Don't bother to explain," Julia cut her off angrily. "I just wanted to tell you that *I* know you're a liar, even if other people believe your stupid stories."

Julia didn't stick around to see their reactions. She pushed past them and walked out of the locker room. Out of the corner of her eye, she saw a couple of girls standing around, mouths agape. Obviously they'd overheard the confrontation. Good. Julia wanted it clear that she had nothing to hide. Courtney was the one with the problem, not her.

She walked briskly down the hallway, smiling at a girl she recognized from homeroom, nodding at her math teacher. But a rage boiled inside her as she replayed Courtney's comment in her mind. She had been feeling like she was a part of the community for the first time since she'd arrived at Sullivan High. Courtney had managed to destroy that feeling in an instant.

Julia walked into her next class, feeling as if the weight of the world had settled on her shoulders. Moments ago everything had seemed so right. Now it was all so wrong.

# Nine

GYM CLASS WAS over, but Austin still felt full of energy. He was revved up from his evening with Julia the night before. She was so special, so different. He had never felt this way about a girl before, and it made him feel on top of the world.

"Hey," he said to Lucas as the rest of the guys started to file out of the gym. "You want to stick around and shoot some hoops? We both have free period next."

"Good idea," Lucas replied enthusiastically.

Austin grabbed a basketball from the equipment closet and began to dribble around Lucas in the now-empty gym. "Your practice play was looking really good at the rally yesterday," he told Lucas. "I think your last season is going to be your best."

"Thanks, man," Lucas said, trying to get the ball from Austin. "Hopefully, I'll leave Sullivan with a bang."

Austin faked a left and then shot the ball through the basket smoothly. "I'm sure you will."

"Thanks for the vote of confidence." Lucas rebounded the ball and shot it right back in the basket before Austin had a chance to intercept. "I was disappointed that you left the celebration early last night."

"I know," Austin said, dribbling the ball once again. "But Courtney was being such a pain. She was making Julia uncomfortable." He threw the basketball up. Brick.

Lucas laughed, grabbing the ball. "She's just jealous. That's the price you pay for being such a stud."

"It is rough." Austin grinned. "I've told Courtney I'm not interested plenty of times. She better just get used to seeing me with Julia."

Lucas dribbled right past Austin and expertly made a perfect layup. "You really like that girl, huh?"

Austin nodded. "Yeah, I do." He retrieved the ball, dribbling slowly.

Lucas exhaled deeply. "I'm not psyched to tell you this, but it's better that you find out sooner than later."

Austin stopped dribbling and held the ball. "What?"

Lucas ran a hand through his hair. "Remember I told you I was going to see what I could find out about Julia?"

Austin took a step back, rolling his eyes. "Yeah, Detective Malloy, I remember."

Lucas looked down at the ground. "Well, I asked around and found something out."

Austin slowly bounced the ball. "Yeah . . . ," he prompted.

Lucas took the ball from Austin's hands. "My friend knows this guy George who went to the same school she did. He says she hung with a pretty fast crowd. She was known to steal stuff."

Austin smirked. "Get out of here! You're playing me, right?"

Lucas shook his head. "No, man. I'm just telling you what I heard."

"Well, I think that all you heard was a stupid rumor," Austin snapped, taking the ball from Lucas and bringing it back to the equipment closet.

Lucas followed. "Listen, I didn't want to tell you this. This is what *I* was told. I'm only looking out for you."

"Lucas, I appreciate your concern. But I think your friend got his wires crossed. Julia's not like that."

Lucas shrugged. "Believe what you want to believe. Just be careful." Lucas started walking toward the door. "I'm going to head to math. See you later."

"See you," Austin called after him. He stood in the empty gym and watched Lucas walk out the door. He'd known Lucas for years—and Julia just a few days. Could Lucas be right? Could Julia Marin actually be a thief?

★    ★    ★

Two classes later Julia practically collided with Austin on her way into the cafeteria. "Julia!" Austin backed away and looked at her with surprise. "Where were you this morning?"

"I was late," Julia answered breathlessly. Thoughts whirled in her mind. Part of her longed to pour out every detail of what had happened in gym class, but something held her back. A little voice in her mind told her to remember how tight Austin was with his friends. Besides, she wanted to forget about Courtney's remarks—just thinking about it made her head pound.

"What's the matter, Julia?"

Before Julia could make up her mind about what to say, Gavin appeared. He gave Julia a quick glance. "Hi, Julia." Then he turned to Austin. "Come on," he told him. "We gotta skip lunch so we can study for the history test, remember? I grabbed us some sandwiches to go. Lucas is gonna join us."

Austin's eyes flickered from Julia to Gavin and back again. "Yeah. Well, Julia, I guess I gotta go." Austin turned to walk with Gavin down the hallway.

"Wait," Julia said to him, hurt. She reached out and touched Austin's arm.

Austin stopped, but so did Gavin. It made Julia feel uncomfortable . . . like being with Austin meant she had to be approved of by all his friends too. And from the way she'd been treated, Julia had the feeling approval had been denied.

"What's going on?" she whispered. "Last night we had—"

"Glad you had a good time," Austin interjected. "Stop by the newspaper office for the meeting after school. You might enjoy it." He started to walk down the hall again. "See you later," he added.

"Later," Gavin called over his shoulder.

Julia stood there, frozen. Austin had sounded so casual, so distant. As if last night had never happened at all. She walked into the cafeteria.

*Get with it, Julia,* she scolded herself as her insides twisted. *You don't know anything about this guy, except that he reads to little kids and that he's incredibly, unbelievably handsome. Everything else is just a fantasy. So get over him.*

Reason wasn't working. Deep down she couldn't shake the feeling that Austin was more special than anyone she had ever known. She just didn't think she could stand it if he wasn't really interested in her.

Julia approached the table where Kayla always sat, and her spirits took another nosedive. Kayla was getting up from the table, and Courtney and Tiffany were standing on either side of her. When Julia drew near them, they all stopped talking.

"See you later, Kayla," Courtney said.

"'Bye," Kayla responded softly.

Courtney and Tiffany walked away without saying anything to Julia.

"What's going on?" Julia asked.

Kayla suddenly got very concerned with stacking her books neatly. "Never mind. It was nothing. Just stupid stuff."

"C'mon, Kayla. What were they talking about?"

"Forget about it. You don't want to know."

Julia stared steadily at Kayla. "I think I do."

Kayla sighed. "Well . . . it's, uh, that . . . that they were telling me I'd better stay away from you because . . . because you couldn't be trusted."

"Go on," Julia prompted.

Kayla took a deep breath. "They said you had a rep as a thief in your old school. Lucas told them that he heard this from some guy named George who went there with you. Anyway, I think Lucas is spreading this rumor around."

"What?" Julia exclaimed. "I don't even know anybody named George!" She felt as if all the wind had been knocked out of her. "Oh, wow," she said softly. She'd thought she'd received a couple of strange looks in her classes, but she'd brushed them off. "A girl who sits next to me in math shifted her purse to the other side of her chair, away from me. She must have heard this stupid rumor!"

"No way," Kayla said sympathetically. "I can't believe that."

Julia slammed her books down on the table. "It's not fair! Between Lucas and those two—" She let her breath out in an explosive burst. "I just don't get it. I didn't do anything to them, but they have it in for me. Kayla, I'm not a thief!"

People sitting at the tables surrounding them

stared. "Calm down, Julia," Kayla said. She sat down, pulling Julia down next to her. "Sit down and chill out for a minute." Her large brown eyes were full of sympathy. Her voice was gentle. "You have every right to be angry. I don't believe a word."

"Thanks," Julia mumbled.

Kayla leaned in close to Julia. "Lucas can be pretty nasty. I'll bet he put Courtney up to this," she said thoughtfully. "She's after Austin. And Tiffany will do whatever Courtney tells her to. She has no mind of her own. That's my take on the situation." She patted Julia's hand. "I'm sure it will all blow over. They're all just jealous because Austin has taken such an interest in you. How are things going with him anyway?"

Julia sighed. "They aren't. I thought they were going great, but I guess I was wrong. Last night everything felt so right. Then when I saw him today he was, like, I don't know . . . distant, removed. All he talked about was a meeting for the paper." She frowned.

Rain had begun to splatter against the windows, and the sky was a leaden shade of gray. At least it matched her mood. "I'll bet Austin heard the rumor," Julia said unhappily. "Lucas probably told him first. That's why he acted the way he did."

Kayla chewed her lip. "Don't jump to conclusions. It's obvious that there's a definite attraction going on between you two. I don't think Austin would change so quickly just because of something he heard." She tilted her head to one side. "If he mentioned the meeting, I think you should go. Then you can scope things out."

Julia shook her head. "I don't think so. I'd feel weird."

"Why? You're just a new student checking out an extracurricular activity: Austin Worth."

Julia didn't respond. Deep in her heart she knew that she *wanted* to go to the meeting, but after Austin was so cold, she wasn't sure that she should.

"Go for it," Kayla urged.

Julia changed her mind about going to the meeting at least fifteen times that afternoon. By the time her last class was over, she had decided that she should definitely skip it. But she found her feet carrying her to the room where the meeting was being held just the same.

Half a dozen kids were already sitting in the empty classroom when Julia arrived. She recognized Jody Case, a girl in her history class. Gavin sat in a corner, doodling. As soon as she sat down, Courtney and Tiffany strolled in. *If Lucas comes, I'm outta here,* she vowed. Then Austin walked in. Their eyes locked for a moment. Julia felt the blood rush to her head.

Whatever Austin's reaction was to seeing her, he wasn't giving it away. He was all business. He slapped a folder on the desk in the front of the room and pulled out a notebook.

"Okay, let's start by discussing the layout for the

edition featuring the pep rally." He opened the folder. "I took a lot of photos, and I need to get some feedback on which shots you think we should include."

Julia was sitting closest to him, and he handed the glossy prints to her first. She had expected them to be focused and competent. After all, he had looked like he knew what he was doing. But what she saw took her breath away: His photos were amazing. There were colorful close-up shots of the football players charging through a whirl of bright pom-poms. Cheerleaders leaping high in the air. The band playing a rousing march. The crowd roaring in the bleachers. Austin had captured every bit of the excitement that was in the air last night.

"Wow, Austin. I mean, these are totally incredible," Julia blurted out, still staring at the photos.

"'Wow, Austin, these are totally incredible,'" Courtney echoed sarcastically, just loud enough for Julia to hear.

Julia rolled her eyes and passed the photos on to the person next to her. She wasn't going to let Courtney get to her.

Austin continued, "Here's the preliminary layout Courtney worked up." He handed out photocopies that showed where all the pictures and stories would go in the edition. Julia took her copy and studied it. The wheels started to turn in her head.

It was all wrong. It was boring. Everything was straight up and down, side by side, in columns that were the same width and length. It wouldn't even have gotten a passing mark in freshman design.

But Austin was moving along. "So that's the layout. Now we still have space to fill—"

"Excuse me," Julia interrupted. "Is this layout final? I mean, can it be changed?"

Austin looked at her with a blank expression. The room got so quiet that you could have heard a pin drop. And if looks could kill, the one that Courtney was giving Julia would have finished her off for good.

Julia stepped to the blackboard without waiting for a reply and began drawing, making columns and circles. "See, if we vary the size of the different elements, we get something that's a lot more interesting to the eye, like this . . . or maybe this."

She was frantically moving the chalk across the blackboard. "Or this. See?"

Courtney was the first to speak up. "Julia, this isn't a basic school paper. It's supposed to look sophisticated, not like a comic book."

"I think we should stick with Courtney's layout," Tiffany said.

"Wait a minute," Jody interjected. "Let's be a little open-minded, guys. What Julia is doing is great. It's a fresh new look. I think we should try it."

"A new look would be nice," the guy who was sitting next to Jody agreed. Julia looked at him for a moment, grateful to get some support. He was tall and gangling, with thick black hair that fell to his shoulders. Julia recalled that he sat toward the back of her history class and that his name was Bill. *Thank you, Bill,* she said silently.

"I have to agree," Gavin added. Julia was shocked that he was taking her side. "It can't hurt to give it a try," he said.

Julia saw Courtney shoot Gavin a poisonous glare. He just shrugged. Julia smiled with satisfaction. She knew she was right.

Soon everybody in the room was voicing enthusiasm about Julia's suggestions. Everyone except Courtney and Tiffany, that is. But they had no choice but to shut up while everyone else jabbered away.

Time flew by, and pretty soon Austin was wrapping things up. "Okay, since we're pressed for time, Julia and I are going to work up the new layouts together. I'll have them copied, and everyone can pick up one from the newspaper's mailbox in the main office next week. I guess that's it."

Courtney made a show of checking her calendar and fumbling through her purse while everyone else started to leave. Julia slowly picked up her books, hoping that Austin would say something to her before she left.

"Julia, do you think you could stay for a few minutes? I'd like to talk about those layouts."

Julia's heart sank a little at his professional tone. "I guess so—if it's only for a few minutes."

Courtney snapped her purse shut with a loud *click* and stomped out of the room. She slammed the door, leaving Austin and Julia alone. Silence hung thickly in the air.

"About the layouts . . . ," Julia began.

"Forget about the layouts."

"What?" Julia asked, confused.

"I mean, the layouts are fine. You can be in charge of them entirely. Just show me what you want by Monday." Austin pulled a chair close to Julia's and sat down. "I just wanted to be alone with you."

Julia angled her body away from his. "I don't get it. You've been acting so different today, so weird. Like when I saw you outside the cafeteria."

Austin looked down at the ground. "I guess I was just freaked out a little."

"I think I can guess why. It was something Lucas said, wasn't it?" Austin looked back at Julia. "Something about my stealing and a stupid story about somebody named George?" Julia felt herself getting worked up again as she spoke.

"Yes," Austin told her.

"I don't even know anybody named George," Julia murmured.

Austin touched her cheek, then gently pushed back a few strands of her hair. "Well, whoever this George is, he must have you mixed up with somebody else. It's a big mistake, that's all. I just got weirded out when Lucas told me." He paused. "I'm really sorry."

"How can you be so sure it was a mistake? You seemed pretty worried before," Julia said stiffly.

"I was just surprised. I got confused for a second. Forgive me?" He leaned in close to Julia, their heads inches apart.

"How do I know that you won't get confused again?" she whispered.

"I won't. I promise," he whispered back.

Julia's pulse was racing. His lips were now so close to hers. *This is it. He's going to kiss me.*

"Ahem." A loud voice suddenly broke in.

Austin and Julia both jumped. A maintenance man was standing in the doorway. He wiped his hand on the sleeve of his gray uniform. "Sorry to bother you kids, but I've got to mop in here. I rapped on the glass, but you didn't pay any attention."

Julia leaned her head back and looked at the ceiling. *What's going on? Did someone up there put a jinx on me?*

Then she looked back at Austin. He shook his head, grinning. "Looks like we're being kicked out of here. Want to go get something to eat?"

"Not at Hot Rods."

"Absolutely not. I know a nice little place where we can be alone."

"You're on."

# Ten

AUSTIN STUCK TO his word. He took Julia to Emilio's, a romantic little Italian restaurant in the center of town. There were red-checkered tablecloths and tall white candles stuck in old Chianti bottles. Soft music played in the background, and waiters moved seamlessly throughout the room.

They sat at a small round table, in a dark, intimate corner. Austin placed his hand over hers. Julia smiled as she watched the candlelight flicker across his face.

"This place is beautiful," she told him. "It's perfect. It's so romantic, it's so—" Julia caught herself before saying anything more. She realized that she was blurting out all her thoughts, and she suddenly felt self-conscious.

"You're right," Austin said softly. "It *is* very romantic." He touched her cheek gently. "That's why I brought you here."

"Ready to order?" The waiter appeared suddenly.

Julia glanced up at the waiter. "I haven't had a chance to look at the menu yet." She smiled, embarrassed.

Austin's lips curled just a little at the corners. "The spaghetti with meat sauce is incredible," he told her. "You want to try it?"

Julia nodded shyly. Austin ordered and handed the waiter their menus.

"I'm glad you brought me here," Julia said softly. She couldn't take her eyes from Austin's face. As she looked at him, she thought back to the bad-boy types she'd fallen for in the past. And now here she was with Mr. Preppy, an all-around good guy.

"What are you thinking?" Austin asked.

"Actually, I want to ask you something." Julia said.

"Shoot."

Julia traced the outline of a square on the table-cloth. "Last time I asked you this, you sort of avoided the question."

"Uh-oh, sounds serious," Austin teased.

Julia smiled. "It's just that you said you read to those kids at the library only to put it on your college applications. I don't believe that." She gave her head a little shake. "It just doesn't sound like you. There has to be something more."

In the glow of the candle's flame, Julia saw that Austin's expression became serious.

"Austin? Is something wrong?"

He took a deep breath. "No, it's just that you caught me off guard. There's nothing wrong with

96

talking about it, really. It happened years ago."
He was talking so softly that his voice was practically a whisper.

The waiter returned, placed two glasses on the table, and poured water from a pitcher. "Can I get you anything else to drink?"

"Not for me," Julia murmured.

"No, thanks." Austin waved him away.

"Please, go on," Julia said gently.

Austin nodded. "I had a younger brother, Scott," he explained. "Actually, nobody ever called him Scott, always Scottie. He was a beautiful kid—always laughing and smiling. He loved it when I read him stories. He wanted to follow me everywhere."

Austin paused, then went on. "You know how jerky guys can be when they're just starting to grow up. Well, when I was in junior high, I never wanted to be seen with my little brother tagging along. I thought it was very uncool." Austin's voice was shaky. He paused again.

Julia took his hand in both of hers and squeezed it. "Maybe this wasn't such a good idea," she said.

"No, no . . . it was. I hardly ever talk about it. It's better that I do." He put his other hand over Julia's.

"Scottie got hit by a car," he continued. "I wasn't around when it happened. I was at school. He saw a puppy across the street, and *bang!* he just ran. My mom said she didn't even have time to realize what was happening. The

97

driver couldn't stop in time." Austin rubbed his hand over his forehead. "I couldn't believe Scottie was gone. I felt numb. And I hated myself for all the times I wouldn't let him come along with me."

"You can't blame yourself. It was an accident," Julia said soothingly.

"I know. At least, I know that now." Austin caressed her hand. "One day I walked into the library and I saw one of the librarians reading to these kids who were about Scottie's age. I went over and asked if I could read. I didn't even think about it, I just knew I wanted to do it. The rest is history."

Julia felt tears forming in her eyes. "I can't believe you went through that," she said in a choked voice.

"It was horrible," Austin told her. "It still is—I think about him every day. But I've always had a lot of support. Especially from Lucas. He was really there for me when all of this happened. He's still always there for me. He helps me to remember Scottie."

Julia nodded. Lucas had obviously been a caring friend to Austin. Maybe the silly rumor about George had been an honest misunderstanding. Maybe Lucas really was only looking out for Austin's best interests.

"Somehow, reading to those kids helped me get through the grief I felt after Scottie died," Austin continued. "It still helps, I guess, though I don't think about it when I'm reading anymore."

Julia heard traces of pain and regret in his voice. She heard the strength and love in it too. "I didn't mean to make you sad," she told him softly.

"You didn't."

The waiter plopped a napkin-covered basket on the table. "Garlic bread!" he announced cheerily. "Compliments of the house!" He bowed. "You'll love it."

Austin rolled his eyes as the waiter scampered away. "Timing isn't exactly this guy's strong point," he said, smiling slightly. He handed the covered basket to Julia. "But the garlic bread *is* awesome."

"If you say so." Julia smiled, opening the basket to pick out a piece of bread. "It does look good."

Austin helped himself to the bread. "Actually," he said, "there's something I've been wanting to ask you."

"I guess that's only fair," Julia responded, taking a bite.

"Well," he began, "it's just that . . . that you never mention your dad. I was wondering where he is."

Julia felt the blood drain from her face.

"You don't have to answer if you don't want to," Austin said hurriedly. "I didn't mean to dig too deep."

Julia shook her head. "No, it's okay. I just wasn't ready for that." She withdrew her hands from Austin's and clasped them tightly together.

"My father was my idol. We always spent a lot of time together. He had a garage in Brooklyn, and

I used to sit there and watch him work. That's how I got interested in cars."

Julia could feel her throat constricting. "One day when I was six, he went out . . . and he never came back. My mother found out that he owed so much money that selling the garage wouldn't have even covered the debts. He liked to gamble, and he had lost everything. I guess he just couldn't face us."

She was clasping her hands so tightly, she could feel her fingernails digging into her skin. "I've never talked about it." A corner of her mouth turned up. "When I was little and my friends would ask where my dad was, I would tell them he had a lot of business trips. I remember one day some kids were over at my house, and one of them said that I was lying. But my mother backed me up."

"That must have been very hard." Austin touched her shoulder.

Julia shrugged. "It was hard for a while. Then I just closed up inside somehow." She sighed. "I made up my mind that I wasn't going to let anything hurt me like that again."

Austin leaned across the table closer to her and spoke in a voice barely above a whisper. "I understand why you'd feel that way. But I hope you won't shut *me* out."

Julia looked into his deep brown eyes, so full of warmth and caring. "I won't."

Austin traced the curve of her cheek with his

100

hand. He leaned close to her until their lips nearly touched. Julia closed her eyes.

"Here you are!" the waiter said heartily. He deposited two overflowing bowls of spaghetti on the table. "Cheese?"

Julia's lip started to quiver. She fought to hold back the laughter. She looked at Austin and saw that he had placed his hand over his mouth.

"Do you want any cheese?" the waiter repeated, louder and more insistently.

Julia and Austin burst out laughing. The waiter looked at them both as if they were crazy, then he shrugged and walked away.

"I am not going to let him keep me from kissing you," Austin whispered, looking into Julia's eyes. She could feel the blood rushing through her veins as he leaned across the small table again.

Usually she hated public displays of affection. Seeing a couple grope each other was embarrassing. But she didn't think about that now. All she could think about was how happy she was. Austin gently cupped her chin in his hand and pressed his mouth against hers. His kiss was strong and overwhelming, but tender and gentle at the same time.

Julia closed her eyes and surrendered to the sweet rush of feelings that swirled around her and through her. They were full of explosions of light and color.

She had been kissed before, but not like this. The others didn't count. This was the only kiss, the real kiss. It made the others seem like the shine of the tinsel tossed in the garbage after Christmas Day.

# Eleven

ON SATURDAY MORNING a week later, Julia was bent over a Chevy engine at the garage when she heard a familiar voice.

"Hey, girlfriend, how're you doing?"

"Hi, Kayla!" Julia grinned and stuck her head out from behind the hood of the Chevy. "Is there something wrong with your car?"

"Nada. You look like you're plenty busy with that engine, though. What are you up to in there?"

"Oh, just checking things out. At first I thought there was something wrong with the starter, but that's not it. Now I'm wondering if it's the transmission. The water pump's not leaking—"

"Whoa! That's enough," Kayla cut her off. "I didn't come here for a lesson in auto mechanics. The real reason I stopped by is because it was a beautiful Saturday morning and I felt like stopping to say hi." She smiled brightly. "How are things with Austin? Did you have a good time with him last night?"

Julia stepped over to the sink and began lathering up. She scrubbed at the grease on her hands and arms. "Yes. We had a wonderful time; it was great. I can't say it enough. Great, great, great, great, great."

"Hmmm . . . so you had fun." Kayla laughed. "Where did you guys go?"

Julia used a clean rag to dry off. "We decided to avoid the usual Sullivan hangouts like Hot Rods and Cinema Village. I just didn't feel like running into his friends."

Kayla tilted her head to one side. "You can't avoid them forever."

Julia chewed her lower lip. "I know, I know. But Austin and I have such a good time when Lucas and Courtney and their whole bunch of followers aren't around. Last night Austin took me to a classical music concert at Academy Hall. Can you believe it?"

A low whistle escaped Kayla's lips. "That's different, I have to admit. Going to see him tonight?"

Julia nodded. Her grin widened. For a brief instant she wondered if her face was going to hurt from smiling too much.

"Listen," Kayla said, rubbing her hands together. "I know you said you want to avoid Hot Rods, but they have dancing every Saturday night. Austin is one incredible dancer. I say if you're lucky enough to have a boyfriend who can dance, take advantage of it."

"Yeah, well . . ." Julia felt the grin disappear.

Kayla opened her eyes wide. "Don't tell me you don't like to dance?"

Julia gave her head a little shake. "No, no. It's not that. It's just that Austin said he'd bring over a video tonight. I thought I'd show him my studio and my paintings, pop some popcorn, and cuddle on the couch with him. My mom's going out with some friends from the office, so we'll have the house to ourselves."

"More just-us romantic stuff?"

"Sure. What's wrong with that?"

Kayla's eyebrows shot up. "Did I say there was anything wrong with that? Not me. If that's what you feel like doing, enjoy yourself." She glanced at her watch. "I've managed to ditch my errands so far, but I'd better get moving. Have fun tonight."

"Thanks, I will." Julia watched Kayla drive away and then got back to work. Sure, it might be fun to go dancing, but she'd rather be alone with Austin. *I'll have plenty of time to try to get along with his friends in the future.*

Austin was due to arrive at seven, but Julia was dressed and had everything ready by six-fifteen. By six-thirty she had fed Gizmo and eaten a cheese sandwich. By six-forty-five she had applied a second coat of mascara. She settled down on the couch to wait, thumbing through a magazine she'd found on the coffee table.

The magazine was one of her mother's and

featured articles on cooking and needlework. Julia couldn't find a single article that interested her.

She put the magazine down and grabbed the remote to channel surf. Gizmo rubbed against her leg and meowed softly. Julia glanced at her watch. It was five after seven. Austin was only five minutes late. Actually, that meant he wasn't late at all when you considered that her watch might be fast.

"Come on, cat," Julia said as she lifted Gizmo to her shoulder. She walked into the studio and examined the order of paintings she wanted to show Austin. She planned to start with the portraits of Itxey and move on to the landscapes and then the abstract stuff.

She looked at her watch again. It was seven-twenty. Twenty minutes counted as officially late—though it wasn't seriously late. Yet.

When seven-thirty rolled around, Julia decided that Austin was indeed seriously late. *He's not going to show,* she thought miserably. *I'm being stood up.* For the first time in nearly ten years, she actually thought she might cry. She didn't.

By eight o'clock Julia was furious. *Who does he think he is?* she fumed. *He could at least call.*

*What if something happened? What if he's being taken to the hospital in an ambulance right this minute?* For the next ten minutes, Julia felt guilty. But by eight-fifteen she was over the guilt and back to being furious.

At exactly eight-twenty, the doorbell rang.

Julia let it ring three times before she answered.

Austin was standing at the door, looking flustered.

"Look, I'm sorry I'm late," he blurted out before Julia could say a word. He held up his hands. "Just *hear* me out before you *throw* me out." He thrust a bouquet of flowers into Julia's hands and walked past her, into the house. He sank down on the sofa and clasped his hands behind his head. "Oh, man."

Julia was losing the firm grip she had on her anger and falling under the spell of curiosity. "So, what happened?" she asked in the most nonchalant voice she could muster.

Austin groaned. "What *didn't?*" He straightened up and gave Julia an admiring look. "You're really something, you know that?"

"Don't change the subject, Austin. You're over an hour late. That should only happen if you're *dead.*"

Austin kept his gaze intent on her. "If I'm dead, it sure feels great." His mouth broke into one of his irresistible smiles.

"Don't even try it. I want to know why you're so late."

Austin got up and took her in his arms. "I'm sorry. I passed by Hot Rods on the way over, and Lucas was outside with Brian Forrest—he's a guy who graduated last year. He's home from college for the weekend. The three of us were really tight, and when we started talking, I just lost track of the time."

Julia pulled away. "Well, that's great, but I

106

started to think that something had happened to you." She folded her arms over her chest. "And you were just hanging out. That's real considerate."

"You're right. I messed up." Austin sighed. "I really didn't mean to. Every time I started to leave, Brian or Lucas started telling me something, and I stayed for a few more minutes. But they're having a party for Brian tonight at Hot Rods and I'm not going, and he's visiting relatives tomorrow. So it was my last chance to see him for a long time. But I still should have called," he said hurriedly.

"Right. You should have." Julia tapped her foot.

"It won't happen again." Austin took her in his arms again. "Forgive me?"

Julia wavered. He sounded so sincere. She had to admit that the pressure of those strong arms had some influence over her too. She drew back and looked up at him.

"Kayla said they have dancing at Hot Rods tonight. Why don't we go? Then you'll be there for your friend's party too."

"No," Austin said quickly. "I don't feel like being around a lot of people tonight. I'd rather just be with you. Alone."

Julia folded her arms. "Are you sure? Dancing would be fun."

"We'll go some other time, okay? Wouldn't you rather it be just the two of us tonight?" he asked as he stroked her hair.

Julia looked into his soulful eyes. "Yes," she told him after a moment. She took Austin's hand and led him into her studio. "Come. I wanted to show you some of my paintings," she explained, gesturing to where her canvases were stacked against the wall.

She decided to let him sort through her paintings at random, picking out whichever ones caught his eye.

He pulled out one of the abstract pictures, a geometric pattern with a background of swirls of color. He turned to her and scratched his head, looking so puzzled that Julia laughed. Then he flipped through several canvases, pulling out one she'd done of the Fulton Fish Market in New York; it showed a man in a cap and sweatshirt weighing a dozen fish in front of a stall piled high with wooden crates. Two other men were also in the painting, carrying a huge fish suspended from a pole. In the background was the market—aisles and aisles of fish on tables piled with ice and people caught up in the whirl of activity.

"This is fantastic," Austin told her as he gazed at the painting. "I feel like I'm right there in the scene."

"It's one of my favorites," Julia said, moving close to him. "About fifteen of us met and walked across the Brooklyn Bridge at sunrise. Then we went to the fish market." She wrinkled her nose. "When we first got there, I thought I'd pass out from the smell. But after I was there a couple of minutes, I didn't even notice it." She smiled, then added, "But when we went for breakfast, no one sat at any of the tables around us."

Austin laughed. "You didn't quite capture the smell in the picture, but that's okay with me." He pulled out another canvas. It was a self-portrait of Julia sitting in a huge overstuffed chair, most of her face hidden in shadow.

"That's you," he said. "Not just the likeness, but the you that's inside." He gazed intently at Julia with what she had come to think of as "the look": that heart-melting, soul-searching, penetrating stare of his. It always made her feel naked—not just physically, but emotionally. Somehow, it wasn't rattling her as much as it had in the beginning. She felt almost comfortable with it.

Austin took her hand in his, warm and close. "This year I've found myself questioning things, feeling restless. Do you know what I mean?"

"Yes," Julia told him gently. "I think it's important that we always keep questioning and keep our minds open, avoid accepting too much."

"You're right," Austin said slowly. "I don't think I realized that before I knew you." He let out a deep breath. "I've grown up so sheltered in this small community, living in the same house, the same town, with the same people, my whole life. My friends have stayed the same. Everyone goes to the same country club, knows the right people. Your life is mapped out for you the moment you arrive in the delivery room at Sullivan General." He let out a short laugh. "You even think you made up your own mind about it."

He looked down at Julia. "You don't just go

109

along with things—you're different. You're a breath of fresh air. I like that."

"I'm glad," Julia whispered. She led him out of the studio and turned out the light.

In the living room Julia popped the video she'd rented—*Dr. Zhivago*—into the VCR, and the two of them cuddled close on the couch.

After a while Austin cupped her chin in his hand, turning her face toward his and kissing her gently. He kissed her again, and then he put his arms around her and pulled her against him, kissing her more passionately. Julia clung to him and let herself be swept deeper and deeper into his kisses. She never wanted the night to end.

# Twelve

*P*ING! *PING!* JULIA woke up the following Saturday morning to the sound of pebbles hitting her windowpane. She went to the window and looked outside. Austin was standing there, looking up at her and holding a palm full of little rocks.

She raised the window and stuck her head out. "What are you doing?"

Austin raised a finger to his lips in a shushing gesture, pointed to his watch, then motioned for her to come out.

Julia nodded. She glanced at the brass clock that stood on her nightstand. It was eight o'clock in the morning! *No wonder Austin didn't knock!*

She pulled on her blue bathrobe with the green stars, raked a brush through her hair, and put on her silk slippers. Then she hurried downstairs.

"Wow," she said breathlessly as she pulled open the door. "How come you're here so early?"

"God, you're beautiful," Austin said without taking his eyes off her. "I just couldn't wait to see you." He grabbed her and gave her a huge hug, lifting her into the air.

Julia threw her arms around his neck and inhaled the smell of his shampoo and aftershave. His lips brushed against her hair before he set her on her feet. "Slow down," she said with a laugh. "I just got out of bed. How about a cup of coffee? I could use one."

Austin nodded. She took his hand and led him inside. "Just try not to wake my mom," she whispered.

In the kitchen Julia brewed coffee while Austin sat at the table. She could feel his eyes on her, watching her every move. Now and then she turned and looked back at him and smiled. It felt so comfortable. So right.

Suddenly she felt Austin's arms around her waist. She leaned back against his broad chest. They stood still, sharing the warmth of each other's touch. "I haven't stopped thinking about you since last night," Austin whispered, his lips so close she could feel his breath against her ear.

"Same here," she said softly. With his arms still around her, she poured the coffee into cups.

"Milk? Sugar?" she asked.

"Black."

"It's strong," Julia warned him.

"So am I," Austin teased, and tightened his arms around her.

Julia shivered. "The coffee is going to get cold," she said after a moment.

"Who cares?" Austin answered.

Julia turned in his arms to look up at him. "I have to get ready for work soon," she said.

"I know. That's why I came early."

Julia studied the planes of his face, the clean line of his jaw, the tender curve of his lips, the way a few wisps of hair fell over his forehead. "I'd like to do a couple of quick sketches of you," she said. "Is that okay?"

"Sure. I'll even take my clothes off." He winked.

"Don't even think about it," Julia said, grinning. "Come with me."

They picked up their coffee mugs and tiptoed into Julia's studio. The morning sun shone through the windows, lighting it with a pinkish golden glow. "You sit here." Julia led Austin to a chair in the corner. "Just get comfortable."

"Are you absolutely sure you don't want me to take my clothes off?" Austin asked, his eyes twinkling.

"Behave." Julia picked up a pad and a piece of charcoal and settled on a stool several feet away. She balanced the pad on her knees and started to draw, making long sweeping strokes.

Her eyes traveled slowly over his face. She made the charcoal lines as if she were touching his forehead, his chin, his jaw, trying to catch the brilliant sparkle of life that shone from his eyes.

As she drew, Austin stared back at her. Julia's skin tingled with warmth. Her lips parted in concentration.

"You're so beautiful," Austin murmured. "I know I said it before, but I want to say it again." He got up and came toward her.

"It's not finished," Julia said, gripping the pad.

Austin rested his hand on the back of her neck underneath her hair. "I won't move until you let me see the drawing."

Julia closed her eyes for a moment. "Fine with me," she said.

Austin kissed her forehead lightly. "Please," he coaxed.

"Okay." Julia held up the picture.

Austin took a step backward. "You're incredible," he breathed. "I can't believe you did that— just like that." He snapped his fingers. "I never knew I was so good-looking," he teased.

They heard the sound of footsteps coming from upstairs. "That's my mom," Julia whispered. "She's up. You'd better go. I don't feel like explaining why you're here so early."

Austin moved his hands down her arms. "Okay. I'll call the garage later." A corner of his lip curled. "My girlfriend, the mechanic." He picked up both of her hands in one of his and held them to his lips. "And the artist."

"You have a charcoal smudge on your face," Julia told him.

"I'll keep it," he said. They heard the sound of

water running upstairs. Julia walked Austin to the door.

"'Bye. I'll talk to you later," she whispered. She smiled as she watched Austin walk out into the bright morning sunshine.

"You look like you're walking on air," Tony said when Julia showed up for work at the garage several hours later.

Julia could feel a smile spreading across her face. "That's exactly how I feel," she told him. She picked up her mechanic's coveralls and stepped into them, pulling them over her clothes. "Ah, romance!" she said, giving Tony a wink.

"Glad it worked out," Tony told her. "But we've got a big day today. Think you can take your mind off that guy for a while?"

Julia tilted her head back and pretended to be thinking things over carefully. "Yeah, I think I can manage."

"Good." Tony led her into the garage. "First job of the day: a new set of spark plugs for the Chevy." He gently rapped on the car's hood.

"No problem," Julia told him.

From then on, the day went by in a blur of adjusting brakes, replacing mufflers, changing tires, and pumping gas.

Julia had just finished replacing a battery when she looked up to see Austin standing in the doorway of the garage, staring at her.

"How long have you been there?" she asked,

flustered. She grabbed a rag and began to wipe the grease from her hands.

Austin gave her a slow smile. "I don't know," he said. "Long enough to see you in action, working. It's like poetry in motion. I never knew a girl could look sexy while she's working on a car." He gave a low whistle. "You sure do, though."

"You're pretty cute yourself," she said, flushing with pleasure. He did look remarkably cute in his khaki pants. And his deep turquoise T-shirt brought out the faintly golden color of his skin and made his eyes look an even deeper brown.

A tingle of anticipation shot through Julia as she thought about how much fun they would have on their date that night. They would have hours to spend together, and then, later, Austin would take her in his arms. He would kiss her, gently at first and then more urgently, just as he had last night. From the look on Austin's face, Julia was sure he was thinking about the same thing.

Julia glanced at her watch. "Wow!" she said. "I've been so busy all day, I didn't realize how much time has gone by. I can go home soon."

She flashed Austin a smile. "I'll just shower off the grease and change, then I'll be ready to go. Maybe we should go to Hot Rods tonight. I like spending time alone, but—"

Julia stopped speaking abruptly when she saw a shadow cloud Austin's features. "What's wrong?"

Austin hesitated. "I'm going to have to break our date for tonight."

"Why?" she asked, a sharp edge of disappointment stabbing in her side.

Austin cleared his throat. "Well, my uncle Glen is in town unexpectedly. My dad wants to take him out for dinner. It's one of those family things."

"Oh." Julia was silent for a moment. "Do you think maybe we could get together after dinner?"

Austin shook his head. "Probably not. We're eating late, then dinner will drag on, and Lucas will be with me—"

"Wait a minute," Julia interrupted, confused. "Why will Lucas be with you?"

Austin's cheeks reddened. "Oh, well, because he's coming to dinner with my family."

Julia stared into Austin's eyes. "Lucas is invited to dinner, but I'm not?" She put her hands on her hips. "Austin, I'm your girlfriend and I've never even met your parents."

Austin walked closer to her and stroked her hair gently. "I know, I know. And I want you to meet them."

"Then why can't I come tonight?" she asked, looking up at him with questioning eyes.

"Lucas has known my family for years," Austin explained. "He's practically my brother. My uncle can be difficult, but Lucas gets along well with him." He squeezed her shoulder. "You wouldn't have any fun, trust me. You'll meet my parents another time, in a more relaxed setting."

Julia looked down at the ground. "If you say so," she said quietly.

Austin cupped Julia's chin in his hands. "I promise you," he told her. He leaned over and kissed her lightly on the lips, then her neck.

Julia felt her anger disappear along with his kisses. "Well, I'm going to miss you tonight," she said grudgingly.

"I'll miss you too." Austin straightened up. His eyes widened. "I've got a great idea. Why don't we go into New York tomorrow and spend the day? I want you to show me all those places that mean so much to you."

Julia smiled. That would be perfect. Her favorite guy in her favorite place. . . . "I would *love* that."

Austin gave her a warm hug. "Terrific. I'll call you early. About eight o'clock?"

Julia nodded, cheered by the prospect of going to the city with Austin. He kissed her quickly on the mouth, then trotted over to his car.

Julia watched him drive away. *Not seeing him tonight won't so bad since we're spending the whole day together tomorrow,* she reasoned.

But in the back of her mind, there was still a nagging feeling that something was not quite right. It was strange that she'd never met his parents. They always hung out at her house, never his. And they spent all of their time alone.

She let out a deep breath. Maybe all it takes is time.

# Thirteen

"I COULD ACTUALLY see your face light up when we got here," Austin told Julia the following day as the two of them strolled toward the East Village in Manhattan.

Julia laughed softly. "It's not just New York that's making my face light up."

They'd parked the Volkswagen in a parking garage, and Julia was bubbling over with the excitement of being in her favorite city with Austin. They'd had a lot of fun on the three-hour drive from Sullivan to Manhattan, singing along to the radio and taking in the beautiful fall day. Austin hadn't mentioned anything about dinner with his family the night before, and Julia hadn't brought it up. She had resolved to free her mind of any negative thoughts and just enjoy herself, which had been pretty easy to do. Julia had never felt more in sync with a guy as she did with Austin. She took Austin's hand as they walked. "You're making me pretty happy too," she told him.

Austin leaned down and kissed her cheek. "I'm glad," he whispered. Julia felt chills go up her spine. It didn't seem possible that she could really be here, in New York, with Austin. It was too good to be true. "So what part of the city are we in?" he asked.

"Downtown—the village," Julia answered. "It's my favorite part of Manhattan." She gestured around to the jumble of brownstones and low-ceilinged shops that lined the streets. "Right now we're in the East Village, which is my most favorite part."

"What's so special about it?"

"I don't know." Julia shrugged as they stopped at a corner and waited for the light to change. "It's where I usually hang out. I guess out of all the neighborhoods, I think this one is the coolest—it has everything. It's stylish and artsy, but also laid-back. And there a lot of new funky boutiques, but there are also plenty of old-fashioned stores and restaurants that have been here for generations."

"Sounds good to me," Austin said as they resumed walking and crossed the street. "Are you going to show me all of your favorite spots?"

Julia nodded happily. "Yes. There are just so many, I hardly know where to start." She stopped in front of a vintage clothing boutique. "Here's where I got that purple dress I wore on the first day of school."

Austin gave her a sexy smile. "You look great in

that dress." He pressed his face against the glass of the store window and peered inside. "You think they got anything in there for me?"

Julia laughed. "No, they definitely don't have any khaki pants or button-down shirts in there." She tugged on his arm and they continued walking.

"Are you saying that I'm too preppy for the East Village?" Austin teased.

Julia shook her head. "No. That's what's great about New York—every type of style is represented here." She giggled. "Besides, as long as you stick with me, you'll fit in just fine."

"I see." Austin laughed. "Well then, I'll just have to stick with you for a long time, won't I?"

"Yes," Julia answered softly, looking down at the sidewalk. She felt a rush of warmth surge through her body. Everything felt so perfect.

Then she looked up and pointed to a small bookstore across the street. "Itxey and I used to go there all the time. They have a lot of rare out-of-print books there."

"Cool."

"This place has the greatest old movie posters," she said, motioning to another store that they were passing. "And this store has got the *coolest* shoes. Check out those red platforms!"

Austin chuckled. "I can see why Sullivan would seem boring to you. There's so much more here."

"That's what I love about this city—there's something for everyone." She stopped in front of a restaurant that looked like an old-fashioned ice cream parlor. "This place has the best egg creams."

Austin looked at her blankly. "What's an egg cream?" he asked.

"You've never had one?"

Austin shook his head.

"Oh, wow. We have to fix that right away." She pulled Austin into the narrow restaurant. There was a long marble counter and red-cushioned swivel stools.

"Julia!" the chubby, gray-haired man behind the counter cried enthusiastically. "It's great to see you!"

"Hi, Benny!" Julia said, beaming. "It's great to be back. I'm in for the day, visiting."

"Wonderful," Benny said. "What can I get for you?"

"Well, this is my friend Austin. He's never had an egg cream."

Benny shook his head at Austin. "That's no good." He grinned. "Take a seat. I'll make two chocolate ones, special for you and Julia."

Julia and Austin slid onto two swivel stools in front of the counter. "This place, along with Benny, is practically an institution," Julia whispered to Austin as they watched Benny prepare their drinks.

Benny was giving them a running commentary as he went along. "Don't you worry, Austin," he said. "There are no eggs in these drinks, just milk, chocolate syrup, and seltzer. So why do they call them egg creams, you ask?" Benny paused dramatically and looked up at Austin. "I have absolutely no idea!"

Benny laughed and set the tall, frothy sodas in front of Julia and Austin. Julia smiled at Austin, eager for him to try the delicious drink.

"Oh, oh, oh," Benny clucked. "I can see you two are lovebirds. It's all over your faces. I'll leave you two alone." Julia blushed as Benny went down to the other side of the counter to take someone's order.

Austin swiveled in his chair to face Julia. "Is it that obvious?" he asked.

Julia felt her heart beat faster. "I guess so," she whispered.

Austin squeezed her leg under the counter. "Good," he said. "I'm glad it is." He glanced around the restaurant. "This place is great," he said. "You *fit* here, Julia." He took a sip of the egg cream. "Mmm. This *is* awesome."

"I knew you'd like it," Julia told him. She took a sip from her own glass. "I really wish you could meet Itxey," she said as she played with her straw. "I called her house last night to tell her we were coming, but her mom said she's visiting her grandmother in Philly this weekend."

"That's too bad," Austin said. He ran his fingers through Julia's hair. "But I'm sure I'll meet her another time."

Julia smiled at the thought of hanging out with both Austin and Itxey at the same time. "Yes, I'm sure you will."

Austin finished his drink, making slurping sounds with his straw.

Julia laughed. "Done already?"

Austin nodded. "It was delicious. So where to now?"

Julia stood up. "There are so many places I want to take you, I hardly know where to begin! I mean, this is just one small area of New York. There's Central Park, and the museums, and you haven't even seen Brooklyn, where I used to live."

Austin stood up next to her, softly caressing the side of her face with his fingers. "Well then, we'll have to come back many more times."

Julia looked up into Austin's deep, intense brown eyes. "Nothing would make me happier than coming back here with you."

Austin kissed her forehead. "Good. It's a deal."

They paid the check and said goodbye to Benny.

"We're not far from Crate," Julia said to Austin as they walked out of the restaurant.

"Perfect." Austin took her hand. "Let's go."

As they headed toward Julia's old school, she continued to point out her favorite spots. She was pleased that Austin seemed genuinely interested in everything that she showed him.

"This is it," she said happily as they reached Crate, an old redbrick building. She looked up at the slightly crumbling exterior. "It'll be locked today," she told Austin. She pointed up to a third-floor window. "That's where I had my favorite painting class."

She turned to face Austin and watched as his eyes roamed the outside of the building. "I'm trying to understand how you feel about the place," he told her. "I'm trying to remember all the things that you told me about it and to picture you in every scene—you know, get the flavor of it."

Julia listened to his words and felt as if they were wrapping themselves around her heart. After a moment she stopped him from talking any more by kissing him tenderly on the lips.

That kiss ignited a slow flame inside both of them. Austin ran his hands over Julia's shoulders and down her arms. He kissed her long and deeply, neither one of them caring that they were in the middle of the sidewalk. For several minutes they were in a world of their own.

Afterward they strolled around SoHo and the West Village, hand in hand. Julia took Austin to some of her favorite art galleries and boutiques.

They stopped in a Middle Eastern restaurant for a late lunch. Julia introduced Austin to the joys of eating falafel, tabbouleh, and fresh pita bread with hummus. She found it exciting to introduce him to so many new tastes and sights; he seemed to enjoy every minute of it.

After lunch they walked over to Washington Square, a small park in the heart of Greenwich Village. They sat down on a bench and watched a couple of street performers. Julia's mind was now telling her what her heart already knew.

*I'm in love for the first time,* she whispered to herself in wonder. *Incredibly, dazzlingly in love.*

# Fourteen

AT LUNCH ON Monday, Julia could hardly wait to tell Kayla about her wonderful Sunday in New York with Austin. Her words kept tumbling out as Kayla sat across from her, nodding and listening.

"I'm so happy that I don't even mind taking a calculus test," Julia concluded with a laugh. "It must be love."

Kayla pushed her spoon around in her chili, but she didn't take a bite.

Julia studied her friend's face. "Aren't you happy for me?"

"Yes, yes, I am," Kayla replied. But Julia noticed that she didn't smile.

Kayla glanced at the corner table where Austin was sitting with his friends. He was staring out the window. "You and Austin are totally together, right?"

"You know we are."

Kayla pressed her lips together. "Well, what do you usually do on your dates?"

Julia drummed her fingers on the table. She sighed. "We go to movies, we go out to eat, he comes over." She knitted her brows. "Where is this going?"

Kayla leaned in conspiratorially. "You tell me you're in love." She glanced Austin's way. "When do you think love extends to eating lunch at the same table?"

"I don't want to eat with Austin's friends," Julia responded with an edge in her voice. "I always eat lunch with you."

"Then why doesn't he come over here? Nobody's going to dis him." Kayla looked at her pointedly.

Julia fidgeted in her chair. "We don't have to be together every minute."

"Julia, you see the guy almost every night, but during school you hardly speak. When you do spend time together, the two of you are always alone. Is that really the way you want it?"

"Well . . ." Julia felt her insides twisting. "Look, I'm in love for the first time in my life, and I'm incredibly, wildly happy. When I try to share it with you, all you do is poke holes in my relationship."

Kayla shook her head. "That's not what I meant to do—I'm just pointing this out." She paused for a moment. "There's something else I ought to tell you too."

"What?"

Kayla bit her lip. "Well, Saturday night I saw Austin at Hot Rods with a bunch of his friends. I wondered why you weren't there."

Julia stared at Kayla numbly. She felt as though she'd just been slapped across the face. "Austin bailed on our plans for Saturday night," she whispered. Her thoughts whirled in confusion. "He told me he was having dinner with his uncle."

Kayla touched Julia's hand across the table. "Listen, Austin might have some sort of explanation. I just thought you should know."

Julia felt shaky as she stood up and picked up her books. "Thanks for looking out for me," she said in a choked voice. How could he have lied to her like that? Julia glanced over at Austin's table. "I've got to go, Kayla," she said, stifling back the hurt. "I'll see you later."

Julia turned around and walked out of the cafeteria. She didn't know how she was going to make it through the day.

Austin sat at his table in the cafeteria, finishing up his lunch. Lucas came over and pulled up a chair. The minute Austin saw his friend's face, he knew something was wrong.

"What's up, bud?" he asked.

"I can't believe you don't know," Lucas said, leaning forward in his chair. "Yesterday was the season opening of Howell's Pumpkins. I waited for a long time, but you never showed up."

"Wow, man, I'm so sorry." Austin shook his head, angry at himself. *How could I have forgotten?*

Austin and Lucas had an annual tradition of going to Howell's Pumpkin Patch on opening day. It had been Lucas's idea. Scottie had always loved to take the hayride out to the middle of the patch and pick pumpkins there. Austin and Lucas would go with him, both admitting that they actually enjoyed the activity themselves. So after Scottie died, Lucas suggested that they still go to Howell's every year, in Scottie's memory.

And they had never missed a year. Until now. Austin didn't know what to say; he felt horrible. "I can't believe I forgot," he groaned.

"Well, you did," Lucas said with an angry edge in his voice. "And when I called your house, your mom said you were out with Julia."

"We spent the day in New York," Austin mumbled. He sighed and shook his head again. "Why didn't you remind me earlier?"

"I never had to remind you before," Lucas responded. "Besides, you're always with that Julia chick. I hardly had the chance."

Austin winced at the way Lucas referred to Julia. But how could he be mad at Lucas? He was the one who'd been a bad friend. "I feel terrible, man. I don't know what to say."

Lucas leaned back in his chair and shook his head. "You're too wrapped up in that girl. It's like your friends don't even matter anymore."

"That's not how it is," Austin argued. "I'll make it up to you."

"Make it up to me by spending less time with *her*," Lucas stated firmly. "I told you she could be bad news, that you should take it slow. But you don't pay any attention to me. I feel like I'm invisible or something."

"It's just impossible for me to believe that Julia would steal anything," Austin explained.

"I'm only trying to protect you, man. I thought my opinion counted for something." Lucas stood up. "She's not worth losing your friends over." He picked up his tray and stalked off.

Austin leaned back in his chair for a moment, watching Lucas walk away. He sighed. Then he slowly got up and walked out of the cafeteria. Julia was so special, so different—unlike any other girl he had met before.

But Lucas was like a brother to him. Austin pulled distractedly on the hem of his expensive rugby shirt. He and Lucas knew practically everything about each other. He had never fought with him like this. He and his friends had always been a tight group. A kind of family.

He looked down at his hands. Lucas had always been there for him . . . especially when Scottie died. Austin felt a pang of guilt as he thought about how he'd unwittingly blown off Lucas at Howell's yesterday.

And Lucas was just trying to protect him, like he always had. If Lucas warned him to be careful, well, wasn't it because he had Austin's best interests at heart? Could there be any truth to the rumors about Julia?

Austin knew in his heart that his friends would never accept Julia, no matter how special he told them she was. And Julia definitely didn't like his friends either. He'd tried to deny it, but he knew it was true. They'd make him choose. The trouble was, when he thought about being without either Julia or his lifelong friends, he felt empty inside.

The way he saw it, no matter which choice he made, he lost.

# Fifteen

AFTER SCHOOL JULIA sat alone in the classroom that was used for newspaper staff meetings. She and Austin had planned to get together there to go over the new layouts for the school paper.

Julia looked down and saw that her hands were shaking. She needed to stay rational. Austin might have a perfectly good explanation for going to Hot Rods on Saturday night.

But her insides churned, as they had been doing all day. She couldn't shake the terrible feeling she had that Austin didn't want her to meet his family or hang out with his friends. He kept her separate from the rest of his life. Like he was embarrassed by her or something.

The door opened and Austin entered. Julia looked into his eyes, and her stomach lurched. Just by looking at his face, she could tell that something was wrong.

"Hi," he said, barely looking at her. He walked to the desk at the front of the room. "Do you want to go over those layouts?"

"No," Julia said. "We have to talk."

Julia saw Austin stiffen. "Okay," he said in a low voice. He sat down on top of the desk.

After the wonderful day that the two of them had shared just yesterday, it seemed strange that things now felt so cold and distant between them. Julia got up and began to pace back and forth.

"How come you didn't tell me that you went to Hot Rods on Saturday?" she asked angrily, looking down to the floor. "Why did you lie?"

Austin let out a sigh. "I didn't lie," he said. "I told you I was having dinner with my uncle—we brought him to Hot Rods. He likes to dance, so we thought he'd get a kick out of it."

Julia walked over to him and stared into his eyes. He couldn't hold her gaze. "You didn't think that maybe I would have liked to come too?" she asked softly.

Austin looked down at his hands. "No, I didn't think of it."

"We've been seeing so much of each other." Julia put her hands on her hips. "And I thought it was special. But I feel like you don't want me to meet your family or hang out with your friends."

Austin stared out the window. "You're making a big deal out of nothing," he murmured.

Julia put her hand under his chin. "Look at me," she said. "I want to go dancing at Hot Rods on

Saturday night," Julia told him. "I want us to go out where everyone else does, just once, as a couple."

Austin hopped off the desk. He leaned against the blackboard and tapped his foot. "Come on, Julia. It was going to be a surprise, but I guess I'll tell you now: I finally got reservations at that new restaurant, Panache, for Saturday night. It wasn't easy."

Julia swallowed. "Cancel them," she said firmly. "We're going to Hot Rods instead."

"I don't like being told what to do," Austin snapped in a tone Julia had never heard him use before.

Julia drew back in surprise. "I knew you weren't telling me the whole truth," she said quietly. Her cheeks rushed with color, and her heart beat with a dull, steady thud. "You're not sure I'm good enough, are you?" she continued in a louder voice. "You don't think your family would like me, and you don't dare offend your friends. That's why we spend all our time alone, isn't it?"

Austin looked away. "That's ridiculous."

Julia stared at him. "No, it isn't," she said hoarsely. "It's true. I can see it in your face."

Austin drummed his fingers on the desk. "You're paranoid, Julia," he said after a moment.

"I'm *not* paranoid! If anything, I was naive before. Where's your spine, Austin?" Julia practically spit the words out. "You can't face having to choose between me and them. You can't stand up to your stupid friends."

Austin's face was pale. He sat there blankly, staring straight ahead.

Julia stamped her foot. "Just tell me the truth. Come on, Austin, speak up!"

Austin got to his feet slowly. He stood for a moment, his hands in his pockets, not looking at Julia. "I'm sorry," he said softly. He walked to the door and left without looking back.

*It's over. It's over,* a voice in Julia's head kept repeating as she drove home. She had gone for a long head-clearing drive after her confrontation with Austin. Then she'd gone to Kayla's for a while, wanting to be distracted. Kayla had tried to cheer her up, but Julia didn't feel any less upset.

"Everything was so perfect," she whispered, Austin's face so clear in her mind. "Why did you have to spoil it?"

A single tear rolled down her cheek. Julia hurriedly brushed it away.

*If I start crying now, I'm afraid I'll never stop,* she thought. She pressed her lips together and swallowed hard. A choked sob rose in her throat.

As Julia pulled into the driveway, she did a double take. A blue sedan was parked in front of her house. Max's car!

Julia glanced at her watch. It was nearly eight. *Wow, I'm so out of it, I didn't even realize how late it is.* What would Max be doing here now?

Julia remembered the look on her mother's face the last time Max's name was mentioned. She was bursting with curiosity.

Julia pulled her car into the garage and hurried

inside the house. Her mother was in the kitchen, filling the teakettle with water.

"Hi, Mom," Julia said.

"Oh!" Julia's mother was so surprised that she nearly spilled the water from the kettle all over herself. She recovered just in time. "I didn't expect you home yet. I thought you were going over to Kayla's."

"I did," Julia said. "I just left."

Max was sitting at the kitchen table. "Hello, Julia," he said, standing up. He was wearing a dark maroon sweater and black trousers. Julia realized she'd never seen Max dressed in anything but greasy coveralls. *He's good-looking in an older guy, distinguished kind of way,* she thought.

Max cleared his throat. "Your mother and I just got back from that new Spanish restaurant, Madrid," he said. "It was nice."

"Oh, yes, it was very good," Mrs. Marin chimed in. "Yes, indeed. The food was simply delicious." She straightened a dish towel. "The place was very pretty. And the food was . . . very good."

Her *mom* and Max were on a *date?* Julia felt a smile begin to form on her lips. "I'm glad you enjoyed it." The three of them stood there, staring at one another. Then the sudden, sharp whistle of the teakettle made them all jump.

Mrs. Marin turned off the stove. "Want to join us for some tea, Julia?"

"No, thanks," she said, not wanting to be a third wheel.

Max glanced at his watch. "I didn't realize the

time. I've got some things to take care of at home. I think I'd better be going."

Julia saw a flicker of disappointment cross her mother's face.

"Don't leave on my account, Max," Julia said hurriedly.

Max and her mother exchanged glances. Max gave his head a single nod. "Thanks, Julia, but I do need to get home."

Mrs. Marin walked over and put her arm through his. "I'll walk you to the door," she said.

"Good night," Max said to Julia.

"Good night." Julia watched as they strolled into the front hall. She couldn't resist a peek at them outside the kitchen window.

She gasped. Her mother and Max were kissing! She turned her head quickly. She sat down at the table, her back to the kitchen doorway.

After a moment her mother returned. There were two bright spots of color on her cheeks, and her eyes were bright.

*She looks at least ten years younger,* Julia thought as she watched her mother glide across the kitchen floor.

Mrs. Marin patted her hair. She poured a cup of tea and sat down beside Julia, still smiling.

"So, how long has this been going on?" Julia asked, her eyes wide.

"Max and I have gone out to dinner a few times. I was going to tell you, but I wasn't sure how you'd feel." She looked at Julia searchingly. "But I have to say, I think it's really turning into something."

Julia clapped her hands together. "That's great! I like Max." She crossed her arms over her chest. "If he breaks your heart, I'll kill him, though," she said with mock-seriousness.

Julia's mom smiled. "I wouldn't worry about that. Max is a perfect gentleman." She sighed happily. "It's all so sudden," she added dreamily. She blushed, laughing. "Listen to me! I sound like a schoolgirl with a crush. But I haven't been so happy in a long time."

"I'm glad to hear that." Julia gave her mother's hand a squeeze. She paused, knitting her brows thoughtfully. "You know," she began, "I can only remember you having a few dates with a couple of guys over the years. . . . There was Seymour, the plastic-surgical-supply salesman. He always brought me candy bars, but his aftershave smelled bad." She and her mother both wrinkled their noses.

"Then there was Stanley, the math teacher who wore that goofy leather cap all the time and had that laugh, you know, like 'haw haw haw.'"

"Oh, Julia, he wasn't that bad." Mrs. Marin tried to keep a straight face. Then she broke out into a smile. "Okay, he *was* that bad."

"Why didn't you go out more?"

"I don't know. Too busy working and going to school to learn something that would pay well and help us have a better life, I guess. I had a young child." She frowned. "I just didn't think about dating much."

The phone on the kitchen wall rang, and Mrs.

Marin got up to answer it. "Of course, Austin. Julia is right here."

Julia's insides churned. She stared at the receiver her mother was holding out to her and shook her head.

A flicker of surprise and confusion crossed Mrs. Marin's face, but she covered it up quickly. "Oh, gosh, I'm sorry, Austin. I asked her to run up to the Pit Stop and get me some aspirin for my headache. I didn't think she'd left yet, but I guess she has. Shall I have her call you when she gets back? . . . Mmm-hmmm. . . . Maybe she should just call you tomorrow; she might take a while. . . . Okay, I'll tell her. 'Bye." Mrs. Marin replaced the phone in the cradle.

She sat down and faced Julia with an inquisitive expression on her face. "I don't want to talk about it, Mom," Julia said shortly.

Mrs. Marin took a sip of her tea. "All right. I'm sorry you two aren't getting along," she said softly. "I won't push you to talk about it, but you know you can if you want to."

"Thanks," Julia murmured. "I think I'll just go to my room, watch some TV, and go to bed. See you in the morning." She kissed her mother's forehead.

"Good night. Remember, if you want to talk . . ."

"I know—you're here." Julia left the kitchen slowly. Her whole body felt heavy as she went upstairs, as if she were dragging herself up each step.

Once she was in her room, she flung herself across her tiger-print bedspread, reached for the phone, and dialed Itxey's number.

The phone rang once, then twice.

"Be home, be home, Itxey," she prayed.

The phone rang a third time, then a fourth.

"Hello?" Itxey answered breathlessly.

"Itxey, I'm so glad you're there. It's Julia."

"Of course I know it's you, you nutcase. Don't you think I know your voice by now?" Just hearing Itxey's bright voice chatter on a mile a minute made Julia smile. For a few minutes they caught up on what was going on with old friends at Crate, then covered just the basics of each other's lives since they had last talked. The way was cleared to get down to business.

Julia propped herself up against a couple of pillows. "Itxey, that guy Austin has been causing me serious grief. Well, not at first—at first, it was awesome."

"Details," Itxey responded. "I need details. Please explain."

Julia gave Itxey a quick rundown of the history of her flash, crash, and burn relationship with Austin. Itxey gave her full attention to every word and never tried to interrupt Julia or hurry the story along.

"Well?" Julia said finally. "What do you think? Don't hold back."

"When did I ever?" Itxey's voice bounced back. "Julia, I'm going to give it to you straight. He's not for you if he hangs out with a bunch of jocks and snobs and chooses them over you."

"But he's not really like that," Julia said quickly.

Itxey faked an exaggerated groan. "I knew it, I knew it. You spent at least fifteen minutes cutting the guy down, but you don't really believe it.

You're s-t-u-c-k, stuck on him still. All I know is what you told me, Julia. I wish I'd been around to see you guys this weekend."

Julia sat up, put her feet on the floor, and leaned her elbows on her knees. "Me too. I'm so confused. I know I'm stuck." She sighed. "But I'm going to get unstuck just as soon as I can."

She twisted the phone cord between her fingers. "Maybe I should come back to New York. I miss it there. I miss school, I miss our friends. I miss you. Everything and everyone here is so different. I know we used to kid about my staying with you, but now I'm serious. Do you think your parents would go for it?"

There was a long silence on the other end of the line. "I'm not sure. Maybe. I'd like it, Julia, and I'll ask my parents about it if you want. There's just one thing I have to tell you that's kind of important."

"Shoot."

Itxey's voice became slightly unsteady. "Well, it's just that I've started seeing this guy now, and I think . . . I think it's going to be the real thing. You know, like . . . love."

"Itxey, that's great."

There was another long silence. "It's just that it's Zeke, Julia. The guy I'm seeing is Zeke. I wanted to tell you when we last spoke, but I just couldn't."

It took a moment for Julia to register what she had just heard. Zeke? Itxey and Zeke? The idea was so weird. It couldn't be true.

"Julia? Are you there?" Itxey's panicked voice

sounded small and faraway. "Please don't be mad at me. I didn't plan it—it just sort of happened."

Julia took a deep breath. "I'm not angry," she said after a moment. "I was just surprised." She swallowed. "It was over between Zeke and me before I left. I told you that."

"I'd hate it if you weren't okay about it," Itxey told her. She paused. "You always said that there wasn't really anything between you two. But you're my best friend, Julia. I would never do anything to hurt you. If you want me to stop seeing him—"

"It's all right, Itxey," Julia interrupted. "You didn't steal him from me. We broke up."

Julia heard Itxey sigh with relief. "I'm so glad you said that. I don't know what I'd do if you were angry. Do you still want me to talk to my parents?" Itxey asked.

"Yes," Julia answered slowly. "I *do* want you to; I want to go back to New York so badly—"

"I hear a 'but' coming on here," Itxey cut in.

"But I can't run away from my problems, as much as I want to. And I can't leave my mom."

"Well, you should at least come visit soon. And let me know ahead of time!"

"Maybe I will," Julia said. Then she smiled. "Or maybe you'd like to come out to lovely Sullivan, New Jersey. We've got wonderful malls here."

Itxey laughed. "You make it sound so inviting."

After she hung up the phone, Julia sat on the edge of her bed, staring into space. The two people she loved most in the world were falling in love, and her own relationship was blown to smithereens.

She was happy for her mom and for Itxey. But she also felt like she was being left out alone in the cold, staring through a window into a room where everyone inside was warm and having a wonderful time.

Julia barely made it to school that Friday. She avoided Austin at all costs. Saturday and Sunday went by in a drab, gray blur. Julia moved through them like she was sleepwalking. At the garage she kept misplacing tools, or else she thought she had misplaced them when they were actually right in her hands.

When she wasn't working, Julia shut herself in her studio. She tried to get Austin off her mind by putting her feelings on canvas. He'd called several times, but her mom just took messages for her.

Julia didn't call him back. She had nothing to say.

# Sixteen

ON MONDAY MORNING, Julia walked through the halls cautiously, searching for a glimpse of Austin but at the same time cringing at the idea of seeing him.

At least Courtney and Lucas left her alone in English class. She had expected a few snide comments from them or, at the very least, satisfied smirks. However, neither one of them paid her the slightest bit of attention.

During lunch Julia looked for Austin in line and at his table, but she didn't see him.

She was sitting at a table with Kayla when suddenly she saw him walking toward her. Her heart jumped into her throat.

"Can I sit down?" he asked.

Julia's throat tightened. She shrugged.

"Uh, I think I'll go sit by the window," Kayla said quickly, picking up her tray.

Julia fiddled with her straw, not looking at Austin.

"I know you must be really angry at me," Austin said after a moment. "You have every right to be. I should have been more supportive."

Julia glanced at him. There were dark circles under his eyes.

"It's just that you caught me at a weak moment. I was feeling guilty for not spending as much time with Lucas as I used to," Austin continued.

He leaned closer to Julia. "My parents aren't the easiest people to get along with. I thought it would be easier for you if we stayed away from them and my friends. I realize now that I was only making it easier for myself by avoiding the issue."

Julia concentrated on sliding her glass of water back and forth on her tray.

"Won't you say something?" Austin asked. He reached for her hand.

Julia pulled it away. "You're a little late in figuring things out," she whispered.

Austin's shoulders sagged. "You're right. But I'll make it up to you."

"I don't think you can," Julia said in a small voice.

"Let me try," Austin told her earnestly. "No more hiding out. If my friends don't like the situation, they're history."

Julia looked at him sharply. "Really?"

"Really. I promise you'll meet my parents soon. And once Lucas gets to know you better and sees how terrific you are, he'll come around. He's just being protective—he cares about me. He's having a party this weekend. Come with me."

Julia drew back. "No way."

"Come on, we'll show everyone that we're a couple. And my friends might surprise us. Maybe it'll be easier than we think."

"I've had enough of your friends, thank you," Julia snapped. She sighed. "Why would I want to party with a lot of people I can't stand and who can't stand me? It doesn't make any sense."

"They won't give you a hard time anymore, Julia. Trust me. Things will be different," he insisted. "I *need* for you guys to get along—it's important to me. And maybe they really won't be as bad as you think."

*I trusted you before, and look where it got me,* Julia thought. But the longer she looked into his brown eyes, the more she wanted everything to work out.

Austin reached for her hand again. This time, Julia didn't pull away.

"At least tell me you'll forgive me."

"We'll see," she said softly.

Julia was surprised the next morning before homeroom when Courtney stopped to talk to her. "Hi, Julia!" Courtney said cheerily to Julia, flashing her a wide smile.

"Courtney? Oh, hi," Julia responded, bewildered. She was so shocked that Courtney was nice to her that she didn't know how to react.

"I love the new look you've given the paper," Courtney said brightly. "You were right. It needed a fresh eye, I guess."

146

"Thanks," Julia responded warily. *What's she up to anyway?* she wondered.

Courtney took on a serious tone. "I know we got off to a bad start," she said solemnly. "I hope that we can just put the past behind us."

Julia blinked rapidly, hardly believing what she was hearing. But Courtney was standing there waiting for an answer.

"It's not so simple, Courtney," Julia replied after a moment. She was about to continue when Gavin stepped up to Courtney and tapped her on the shoulder.

"You look hot today," he said. "Cool dress."

"Oh, thanks, Gavin. You're so sweet." Courtney glowed.

When he was gone Courtney turned back to Julia. "I just knew we could start with a clean slate," she beamed. "See you in English!" She sauntered away happily, her blond head bobbing up and down in a sea of other heads.

"I never said I forgave you," Julia whispered. She was still reeling from the encounter when Tiffany came up to her.

"Listen, Julia," she said with a quiver in her voice. "I wanted to tell you that I'm really sorry about what happened in the locker room that day. It was all a big misunderstanding."

Julia fiddled with books in her locker. She could feel Tiffany's eyes on her, waiting for a response. "It's nice of you to apologize for what Courtney said," Julia finally told her. "But I know what I heard—and I don't think it was a misunderstanding."

Tiffany blushed. "B-But it was," she stammered. She sighed heavily. "You must think we're awful," she added.

Julia turned from her locker. Tiffany really did look sorry. Julia didn't think that Tiffany was as capable of putting on an act as Courtney was. Besides, Tiffany wasn't the one who was spreading rumors about her; she just had poor taste in friends. "Well, it's over now."

The look on Tiffany's face showed she was hoping for more complete absolution. "I'm really sorry," she said softly. Then she walked away, disappearing into the crowd.

When Austin met her moments later to walk her to homeroom, Julia couldn't wait to tell him what had just happened. "Courtney and Tiffany apologized to me. I think I've fallen into one of those parallel universes where everyone looks the same but things are different."

"Great," Austin said without batting an eye. "I told you they weren't such a bad bunch. It just took them a little time to come around," he said with a slight toss of his head.

Julia gave him a sidelong glance. "Somehow, I get the definite feeling that you had something to do with this sudden turnaround."

Austin nodded. "I must admit that my charm and powers of persuasion had something to do with it." He flashed Julia a smile. "It was easy," he told her with a shrug. "I just had to explain some things to them. Like the fact that you're more important to me than any girl has ever been before. Also, I know you better than anyone else, and I know those stories about you stealing aren't true."

One side of Austin's mouth turned up slightly into a smile. Julia thought it made him look positively angelic. "Things will be different from now on. You'll see. Believe it."

Things were different, all right. That day at lunch Austin asked Julia to sit at the table with his friends. When she hesitated, it was Courtney who wouldn't take no for an answer.

"Did I hear you right?" Kayla asked when Julia told her why she had sat with Austin's friends at lunch that day. "Courtney Kendall *insisted* you sit with her?"

"I know it's too weird, but I figure I ought to give them a chance, right? You're the one who told me I can't avoid Austin's friends forever."

"I know, but those three really did an about-face, and overnight too." She shrugged. "I guess you've got to go for it. Just be careful to watch your back."

"I will," Julia promised.

Kayla's cautionary words only underscored the uneasy buzz in Julia's own mind. But as time went on, Julia became less and less suspicious. Courtney and Lucas kidded around with her in English. And every minute she spent with Austin was dazzlingly, romantically perfect.

"What are you going to wear to the party?" Kayla asked Julia as they were shopping Wednesday afternoon. It was Julia's first trip to a mall, and she felt like she had to check out every single store.

"Well, Austin said it was casual—but, like, not too casual. No jeans. I guess I'll wear a dress or a skirt."

"How about this?" Kayla thrust a fuzzy, short-sleeved sweater in front of Julia's face. It was exactly like one Courtney wore.

"No way," Julia told her.

Kayla laughed. "Just kidding."

They went to three more stores before they hit Top It Off, a shop that sold only sweaters and shirts. "This is the one," Julia said as she showed Kayla a stretchy, lime green ribbed top. "I've got a great skirt that will go with it. What do you think?"

"It's nice. It will look great on you."

"Thanks." Julia paused a beat. "I wish you were going to the party."

"I do too, but my brother doesn't fly home for the weekend very often. I want to spend every minute I can with him."

"I know, I know. But I still wish you were going to be there for moral support."

"I'll be with you in spirit." Kayla looked thoughtful, then added, "Just be careful, Julia. I still think it's too soon to trust Lucas and company, but I hope I'm wrong."

"Me too."

# Seventeen

"I DON'T BELIEVE this place," Julia whispered in awe as she and Austin stood waiting between the columns that stood on either side of Lucas's front door.

"It's just a house."

"Easy for you to say. Yours is practically exactly like it."

Austin smiled. "Yeah, but mine doesn't have a swimming pool out back."

The door opened slowly. Julia's jaw dropped. "A maid," she whispered.

Austin gave her hand a quick squeeze. "No big deal," he told her. "Hi, Annie," he said to the housekeeper.

"Hello, Austin," Annie greeted him with a smile. "You know the way."

"Certainly do," Austin said. He took Julia's hand, leading her into Lucas's house. Julia's head swiveled this way and that. As they walked under a huge crystal chandelier, Julia felt like she'd fallen into *Lifestyles of the Rich and Famous*.

"They sure have some sound system in here," she remarked. "That music sounds like a live band."

"It *is* a live band," Austin replied.

"Hi, you guys!" Lucas greeted them. He was wearing dark trousers and a matching dinner jacket.

Courtney wasn't far behind him. She wore a short burgundy velvet dress and silver shoes. "Hi," she said. Julia felt the muscles in her neck tighten as she saw Courtney look her up and down.

Austin frowned. "You told me this party was casual."

Lucas grinned. "It *is* casual. You don't see any formal gowns here, do you?"

"Come on, you know what I mean. I didn't think I was supposed to wear a dinner jacket or a tie or anything."

"And you don't have to, buddy. You can wear whatever you like. Seriously, I meant casual cocktail party attire. I'm sorry if we got our wires crossed." He glanced at Julia. "Just forget about the way you're dressed."

"That will be kind of impossible," Julia murmured. All the other girls at the party were decked out in expensive designer dresses and jewelry that was the real thing, not costume.

"Yeah, it's no big deal," Courtney said with a fake-sounding, sugary-sweet tone in her voice. "Oh, there's Mimi. Look how great she looks!" she exclaimed, pointing to a blond girl in a long black gown. "I'm going to say hi to her." Courtney then sauntered away.

Austin looked at Julia and shrugged. "So we're a little underdressed. *You* look great. Just enjoy yourself."

"Right," Lucas echoed, but the expression on his face was far from reassuring. Then he began to talk to Austin about the last football game. Julia listened politely, looking from Austin to Lucas, depending on who was speaking. She knew next to nothing about sports, so she couldn't jump into the conversation.

After a few minutes of smiling and nodding, she was completely bored. She drifted over to the punch bowl. She took a sip of the bright pink concoction. It definitely contained something stronger than punch. She put her glass down in disgust. A few people glanced her way. None of them came over to talk, however.

Julia walked over to the table where the spread of food was laid out. She took a napkin and picked at a couple of pieces of cheese, but she wasn't really hungry. Then she smiled to herself, realizing that Itxey would be extremely amused if she could see her at this stuffy formal party.

She suddenly felt Austin's arms around her waist.

"Hi there," he said softly into her ear.

"There you are." Julia turned around to face him. "I was getting a little lonely without you."

"I just have to go make a quick phone call." Austin massaged her shoulders. "I'll be right back. But try to have fun, get to know everyone." He kissed her cheek.

Julia decided to walk over to Gavin, who was standing nearby. He had always seemed to be one of the more harmless ones.

Gavin was talking with a dark-haired girl she'd seen him with a couple of times at school and a very tall guy she didn't know.

"Hi, Gavin," she said, and looked at his two friends. "Hi. I'm Julia," she greeted them, managing a smile.

"Hi, Julia," Gavin said, looking at her briefly. "This is Brittany and Garth. Garth has been living in Paris for a year."

Julia nodded. "I'd love to go there someday. I've heard it's beautiful."

"It is," Garth and Brittany said in unison.

"I go there every summer with my parents," Brittany added.

There was a moment of silence. Then Garth shrugged and turned back to Gavin.

The three began chatting about their various experiences in France. Julia listened for a few moments, nodding politely and feeling more and more uncomfortable. None of them seemed to notice when she drifted away.

She thought about approaching another group, but everyone seemed so caught up in each other that she didn't feel like trying again.

*I haven't felt this out of place at a party since Johnny Weaver's when I was six,* she thought as she looked around at the group. Johnny Weaver was a little boy who had lived down the street from Julia when she was growing up. He'd had a crush on her and had invited her to his birthday party. She was the *only* girl he had invited. By the time the party had rolled around, Johnny's crush had worn off, and he didn't say a word to her the whole afternoon.

She sank into a chair in the corner of the room, putting her purse on the table beside her and scanning the room for Austin. He was across the room with Courtney, who was whispering something in his ear. The look on Courtney's face was definitely flirtatious.

Julia's shoulder muscles tightened. *How much longer until we can get out of here?* she wondered. It already seemed like they'd been at the party practically forever.

She got up and took a stroll over to a table covered with bottles of soda. She helped herself to a cup and some ice, then debated over which soda to pour. *Coke or Sprite? Or maybe iced tea?* she asked herself, as if this were the most important decision of her life. She finally decided on Sprite.

When she couldn't possibly kill one more minute, she turned to go back to her chair. On the way over, she saw Courtney and Lucas and some other guests involved in some commotion.

"It's my diamond tennis bracelet!" Courtney was shrieking. "The clasp was broken, so I took it off. I definitely remember putting it right here." She pointed to the table next to the chair in which Julia had been sitting.

Julia could feel the hair on the back of her neck stand up. A siren inside her brain started to go off.

Lucas locked eyes with her. If a picture was worth a thousand words, then the look on his face spoke volumes. Julia could feel the whole situation coming into focus: Lucas had asked her to the party to set her up, and Courtney was in on the plan. In one minute he was going to accuse her of stealing Courtney's bracelet.

The faintest trace of a smile flickered across Lucas's face before he spoke. "We already know who was sitting beside this table. That gives us a pretty good idea of what happened to the diamond bracelet."

Lucas snatched Julia's purse off the table and twisted open the clasp. With a quick flick of the wrist, he turned the bag upside down. The entire contents clattered out: keys, makeup, address book, pen, mints—and Courtney's diamond tennis bracelet.

Julia's pulse raced. She couldn't believe that this was really happening to her.

Lucas stalked over to Julia. "How could you come into my home and do this?" Lucas yelled angrily. "My friends and I tried to be nice to you. We took you into our crowd."

"The rumors were true," Courtney sneered at Julia as she yanked her diamond bracelet from the table. "You *are* a klepto."

By now all the other conversation at the party had died out. All eyes were on Julia. Lucas turned to Austin. "Still think you know her so well?"

*Say something, Austin,* Julia prayed. But Austin just stared at her with a look of confusion and disbelief.

"Are you going to defend your girlfriend now, Austin?" Courtney chimed in.

"I'm not putting up with this another minute," Julia snapped. She wasn't going to stand there while people accused her of being a criminal. She could practically see the joy in Courtney's face as she walked by her to grab her purse. Julia gathered up the contents, shoving them back into her bag. Then she headed for the door.

She almost forgot that she had to ask the maid for her coat.

While she waited for Annie, she listened for Austin's footsteps. But all she heard was the irregular, pounding beat of her broken heart.

# Eighteen

AUSTIN SAT ALONE amid the debris of the party. The guests were gone, and the band was nearly finished packing up. He watched as the caterer's cleaning crew bustled around, breaking down buffet tables and carting out trash. He'd spent most of the party by himself, lying down upstairs in Lucas's room, trying to make some sort of sense out of the situation. He hadn't been able to. "There's something kind of dismal about looking at the mess left after a party," he said as Lucas passed by. "Maybe it's just my mood."

Lucas plopped himself down in a chair beside Austin. "I think it turned out to be a pretty successful bash, don't you?" he said lazily.

Austin snorted. "No, I think it stank."

"Hey, what's bugging you?" Lucas picked up a champagne bottle from the floor and drained the last few drops into his mouth.

Austin sat up straight. "Are you kidding me? Sometimes I wonder if you think about anyone but yourself. After that whole scene with Julia, how can you tell me the party was great?"

A member of the cleaning crew picked up the empty champagne bottle. "Here's a fresh one, fella," he said, depositing an unopened bottle on the rug next to Lucas's chair.

"You don't need that," Austin said, reaching for the bottle.

Lucas waved him away. Austin watched as he peeled the silver paper away and popped the cork with a single, deft motion. Champagne exploded out onto the rug and ran down the side of the bottle in a frothy fizz. Lucas grabbed Austin's glass and started to pour.

"Hey, no thanks," Austin said as he pulled the glass away. "You really ought to lay off the stuff yourself. The party's over, remember?"

"Don't be such a drag. My parents aren't coming home until tomorrow." Lucas filled his own glass and took a gulp. "A little more champagne will cheer you up." He picked up Austin's glass and filled it this time, then handed it to him. Austin put it down.

"Ahhh, be a drag if you want," Lucas mumbled. "Listen, as far as Julia is concerned, I've told you before—good riddance. We all knew she was bad news. When my bud in New York found out she had a bad rep at her old school, I hoped the girl had changed her ways, for your sake. Obviously she didn't. You don't

159

need somebody who's going to lift the family silver when you invite her home to meet Mom."

Austin rubbed a hand over his eyes. "I can't believe she stole Courtney's bracelet."

"Believe it, Austin. It was in her purse. How else would it get there?"

"Yeah, yeah, it was in her purse . . . but it's all so strange. It doesn't add up." Austin leaned forward. "Did you ever find out what happened to those crystal candleholders you got for your mom?"

Lucas hiccuped. "She loved them. Mom has always been a sucker for crystal. She was afraid something might happen to them with all the people around for the party, so she took them upstairs. Want to see them?" he asked, reaching for the bottle of champagne.

Austin grabbed it first. "Slow down on the champagne, Lucas. I'm missing something here. How did you get hold of the candleholders? Did Max find them, after all?"

The look in Lucas's eyes was vague and unfocused. "What's Max got to do with it?" He slurred his words slightly.

Austin narrowed his eyes suspiciously. "You said you called Max when you found they were missing. The last time you saw them, they were in the glove compartment when you took your car to the garage, right?"

A red flush spread from Lucas's neck to his hairline. He reached for the champagne again. "When the candleholders weren't in my glove compartment, I thought Julia took them. Then I found them in my room. I had just forgotten that I had brought them into the house." Lucas smiled sheepishly.

Austin shook his head. "Why didn't you say something?" he demanded.

Lucas shifted his feet. "Because the girl was all wrong for you, and I couldn't get you to see that." He hit the arm of the chair with his fist. "You changed."

Lucas gave Austin a blurry-eyed stare. "I knew when you didn't pay attention to what I said that she had your head twisted around. I remembered how I thought she stole the candleholders, and I got an idea."

Austin stared at him, openmouthed. "But you knew she wasn't a thief all along."

"What's the difference? You're my closest friend. I had to do something to wake you up." Lucas put his hand on Austin's shoulder.

Austin shook it off. "So you decided to wreck my relationship with the girl I love? Thanks, *pal*," he said sarcastically. He stood up and began to pace back and forth.

"Hey, you'll wear out the rug," Lucas joked, trying to make light of the situation.

"What about Courtney's bracelet?" Austin demanded. "It was all a setup, wasn't it?"

Lucas shrugged. "I don't know about that, man. You'd have to ask Courtney."

Austin threw his hands up in the air. "Oh, come off it! After what you just told me, you expect me to believe that you had nothing to do with this?"

He was about to walk out of the room when he noticed that Tiffany was standing in the doorway, her face streaked with tears. "Tiffany? What's going on?"

"I've been driving around since I left the party," she said quietly. "I couldn't stand to go home. I feel awful."

Lucas opened his mouth to speak

"Don't say anything, Lucas!" Austin snapped. "I want to hear what Tiffany has to say."

Tiffany sank into a chair. "The whole thing about Courtney's bracelet was a lie."

Austin's eyes narrowed. "Go on."

She looked nervously at Lucas. "It was part of Lucas's plan to spread rumors about Julia being a thief, a cheat. He convinced Courtney and me to go along. Courtney figured that with Julia out of the picture, she'd have you for herself."

"She'd be a lot better for you than that freak," Lucas muttered.

"Shut up, Lucas," Austin hissed.

Tiffany wiped her red eyes with a crumpled tissue. "I feel horrible for going along with it," she said miserably. "I'm so sorry I didn't say something sooner."

"Quit whining," Lucas told her. He looked at Austin. "We had to do something. You were spending all of your time with that girl. You and I weren't hanging out like we used to. It was all for your own good. I was only looking out for you."

"Oh, man, you're totally twisted!" Austin exploded. "You weren't looking out for me at all. You just wanted to call the shots." Austin shook his head incredulously. "You're sick, Lucas, really sick."

Lucas stood up quickly and staggered sideways. "You can't talk to me that way! We've been like

162

brothers. Don't you remember how I used to beat up the guys who picked on you when we were kids?"

Austin's face had gone pale. He shot Lucas a look that was a mixture of pity and contempt. "God, I feel like I'm seeing you for the first time. How could I have been so blind for so long?" He strode toward the door, then looked back over his shoulder.

"You know, Lucas, you didn't beat up those bullies for me. I think you did it because you enjoyed beating them up." He turned his back and kept on walking.

"Hey, wait a minute. You can't walk out on me!" Lucas called after him.

"Oh no?" Austin challenged. Then he walked out the door, slamming it behind him.

That night, Julia sat in her studio, brush in hand, staring into space. Her mother was out with Max, and Julia took advantage of the empty house by cranking the music up full blast.

*I should have listened to Itxey,* she thought. *Austin is just like his friends, a snob. A jock with an attitude.* She burned with anger as she thought about how Lucas had dumped the bracelet out of her purse. And she got even angrier when she thought about how either he or Courtney must have planted the bracelet in her bag in the first place. She didn't know people were capable of sinking so low.

*Austin didn't even try to defend me,* she thought. *How could he have believed I would steal Courtney's bracelet?* Tears of rage stung her eyes. She flung the brush into a corner and buried her head in her hands for a moment. When Julia lifted her head up again, she was no longer crying. They weren't worth it.

"You're the worst of them all, Austin," she whispered aloud. "I wish I'd never have to see you again."


Austin stood outside of Julia's house, ringing the doorbell. He could hear loud music coming from the studio.

"Answer the door," he pleaded aloud, ringing the bell again and again. When Julia still didn't answer, Austin walked to the back of the house. He saw Julia through the studio window, sitting in front of a canvas. He tapped on the glass with his keys. Julia glanced up from her canvas and looked at Austin with a cold stare.

"Turn down the music!" Austin yelled at the top of his lungs. He motioned for her to open the window.

Ever so slowly, Julia walked over and raised it. She leaned out. "What do you want?" Her breath froze into little clouds in the air.

"Can I come in?"

"No."

Austin sighed. "Julia, listen to me, please. Lucas and Tiffany told me the whole story. I know that you were set up."

Julia gave him a chilly smile. "It's nice that you finally realized that. Now if you're finished, please go away."

"No, I won't go away. We have to talk. Look, I know I was wrong, but try to understand. Lucas has been my friend since we were kids. I didn't want to believe he would lie to me."

"You believed I would, though. You believed I was a criminal." Julia's eyes flashed. "I was humiliated in front of all the people at that party. You just stood there and let it happen. I'm sorry, Austin, but I don't understand at all."

Austin looked deep into her eyes. "You have every right to be angry. Please . . . isn't there anything I can say? I know I was wrong, and I'd do anything to change what happened. I should have defended you. I was being pulled in two different directions."

Julia put her hand on the window frame. "Well, now you won't feel pulled in two directions at once. Lucas and Courtney can have you, with my blessing." She closed the window, leaving Austin outside in the cold.

# Nineteen

"U H-OH," TONY SAID to Julia as soon as she arrived at the garage on Sunday. "I know that look. There's something wrong."

Julia made a halfhearted attempt at a smile. "I guess I didn't realize that my face is so easy to read," she said. She put her hands on her hips. "So, what have we got to do here today?"

Tony tilted his head. "Let's see. I think it'll be kind of slow. Max just finished a tune-up, and I just realigned the brakes on the old Caddy over there. I'm afraid it's pumping gas and cleaning windshields for you unless something comes up."

Julia groaned. "I was hoping we'd be busy."

Tony gave her a long look. "You look like one unhappy camper. Come on into the office. We'll have a cup of coffee, and you can tell me what's the matter."

Julia hesitated.

"Come on," Tony urged. "It's better to talk

these things out." He started toward the office and motioned for her to follow.

Inside, he poured them both steaming cups of coffee from the pot on the hot plate. He took a seat and propped one foot up on the scarred wooden desk that was covered with papers. "Where's Max?" Julia asked. She pulled up a chair on the other side of the desk.

Tony smiled. "As soon as he finished the tune-up, he ran out of here. He said he was going to grab a shower before he met Ann—your mom—for Sunday brunch."

Julia snapped her fingers. "Right. Mom mentioned it. It just slipped my mind."

"Your mom and my dad have been seeing a lot of each other."

"Yeah, they have."

"I think it's serious. How do you feel about that?"

Julia stared into her coffee. "I think it's great." She looked up at Tony. "Oh, you don't think I mind? I'm thrilled for my mom—and for Max too."

Tony took his foot down and leaned across the desk. "Then what is it? The boyfriend?"

"Ex-boyfriend," Julia corrected him quickly.

Tony gave a low whistle. "I had a feeling I was in the ballpark. So what happened?"

Julia wrapped her hands around the coffee cup tightly, sighing heavily. "All right." She poured out the story of what had happened at the party.

"That stinks," Tony said when she finished. "They're a dumber bunch of spoiled brats than I thought."

"Yeah, well, *I* was dumb to fall for the whole thing. I feel like a jerk."

Tony patted her arm gently. "You're not the jerk and you know it."

Julia slapped the desk with her hand. "It just makes me so mad that Austin stood there and didn't do anything. He didn't come after me. I was so embarrassed, and he just let me walk out of there alone." Julia twisted a strand of her hair. "He came by later to apologize, *after* Lucas confessed to everything."

She bit her lower lip. "I just couldn't listen to him. I wanted him to trust me and to stand by me. That apology was worth nothing."

Tony got up and poured himself more coffee. He held the pot out to Julia questioningly.

"No, thanks, I've had enough," she told him.

When Tony sat down again, he looked at Julia thoughtfully. "Friends are important to everybody in high school—especially to guys. A guy's best friend can be closer than a brother." He put his feet up on the desk again and leaned back in his chair.

"I've heard all this stuff from Austin already." Julia turned her coffee cup around and around in her hands. "Did anything remotely like this ever happen to you?"

Tony nodded. "Sure. As a matter of fact, it's the kind of thing that happens a lot. I made some pretty dumb moves too—and I don't think I wised up as fast as Austin did."

Julia looked at him quizzically. "What happened?"

Tony rubbed his hands together. "My best friend was this guy, Steve. We were part of a group of guys that used to do everything together. Then when I met my girlfriend, I quit hanging out with the guys to be with her. That didn't sit too well with Steve."

"So . . . ?"

"So, Steve would get on my case, telling me I shouldn't be spending all that time with one girl, questioning my friendship, that sort of thing. Eventually I caved in and told my girlfriend I had to spend less time with her and more time with my friends. That's not what I really wanted, but Steve's opinion was very important to me at the time."

"What happened?"

"I acted like a jerk—I wasn't nearly attentive enough to my girlfriend. She got pretty mad and dumped me. That hit me hard. And I realized that if Steve was a good friend, he'd understand how important she was to me." Tony shook his head. "I didn't think I'd ever get her back, but after a long time, and a lot of begging, I did."

"Really?"

Tony smiled. "Yes. As a matter of fact, you've met her."

"I have?"

"Yep. That was Amy—my wife."

"Wow," Julia said. She twirled a lock of her hair around her finger thoughtfully. "That's quite a story."

Tony nodded. "Uh-huh. Look, I'm not saying you'll end up marrying this guy. All I'm saying is that you should cool off and think things over before

169

you decide this guy doesn't deserve another chance. If you decide he doesn't, well, all right. Just give it some thought."

Julia took a sip of coffee. "I appreciate the talk. I'll think about it, but I doubt I'll change my mind."

The bell signaling the arrival of a car at the gas pumps sounded. Julia stood up. "Thanks again. Gotta go." Julia looked at the car that had pulled up. She turned back to Tony. "That's not a customer. It's your father's car. He and my mom are walking over here. I wonder what's going on?"

Tony swung his feet off the desk and grinned. "Let's go see."

Max and Julia's mother were standing outside, beaming.

"Hi, guys," Max said heartily.

"I thought you two were going to brunch," Julia said. Her heart started beating faster. Something was definitely up.

Max took her mother's hand. "We never made it to brunch. I couldn't wait." His eyes were sparkling.

Julia looked from Max to her mother. Her mother's face was lit up as if she had just been told she won the lottery. Thoughts whirled in Julia's head. *What is this about?*

Mrs. Marin's smile widened. "Max asked me to marry him," she burst out. "Isn't it amazing?"

Julia's mouth dropped open.

"All right!" Tony exclaimed.

"By the way, she said yes." Max laughed.

Mrs. Marin came close to Julia. "Are you okay with this?" she asked.

"Absolutely! I'm more than okay—I'm thrilled!" Julia threw her arms around her mother and hugged her tight.

The rest of the day passed in a dizzying blur. In all the excitement of her mother's news, Julia found that she was sometimes entirely able to forget what had happened at Lucas's party. She and her mother spent the afternoon calling friends and family, eager to share their good news with everyone. They even began to plan the wedding. Her mother didn't set a date, but she did decide that it would take place in Brooklyn. And Julia eagerly agreed to be her mother's maid of honor. Julia was thrilled to see her mother so happy—she deserved it more than anyone.

Yet as Julia lay in bed that night and thought about her mother and Max's engagement, it did seem slightly surreal. Max would be her stepdad soon! Things were definitely going to be different. It had been just her and her mom for so long. But as Julia closed her eyes and snuggled under the covers, she thought about how happy Max made her mom, and a smile formed on Julia's lips. This was going to be a good change—she was sure of it.

Julia's smile disappeared quickly as she walked through the doors of Sullivan High the next morning. Today she would have to face all the kids who had been at the party, plus all the others who knew what happened—which was probably most of the school. But the worst part of it all was that soon she would have to face Austin. Her stomach twisted into a tight knot.

As Julia made her way through the throng of students in the hallway, her eyes and ears were alert. Without looking right or left, she could feel heads swivel her way as she passed. Her ears picked up snatches of conversation that she couldn't help thinking were all about her and the scene at Lucas's party.

Julia felt her cheeks get hot. She tried to keep herself from blushing or giving the slightest sign that she cared what was going on. *Just plaster a smile on your face and keep your head up*, she coached herself.

When she saw Kayla waiting for her by her locker, Julia had never been so happy to see someone in all her life.

"Good for you, girlfriend." Kayla squeezed Julia's arm. "After I spoke to you last night, I wasn't sure you'd come today. I'm glad you're here."

"I'm starting to wonder why I am," Julia said as she dialed her locker combination. "I don't know if I'll make it through the day."

Kayla smiled gently and put a hand on Julia's arm. "You'll make it. You're not alone. Anyway, I've got some good news. I spoke to Austin."

Julia's stomach lurched. "I don't see how that could be good news." Her hand trembled on the combination lock.

"I saw him in the parking lot this morning. He

said he wanted to talk to you but that you refused to talk to him anymore."

Julia swallowed. Her throat felt dry and fuzzy. "What could he possibly have to say?"

"He said that he and Tiffany are on your side. They'll tell everyone the real story."

Julia smiled tightly.

"Like anyone will pay attention."

"Are you kidding? Like anybody *won't*. Lucas and Courtney aren't exactly known for being trustworthy. Without Austin on their side, they don't have much of a story. And with Tiffany going against Courtney for the first time in her life—well, my guess is that not one person will believe them."

Julia shut her locker. "Do you really think so?"

Kayla nodded solemnly. "Yes, I do." She paused a beat and then added, "You know, Austin really sounded sorry."

Julia tossed her head. "Good for him. If he had trusted me in the first place, he wouldn't have to be sorry."

Kayla shifted her books. "I can see why you're angry and disappointed, Julia, but he was in a bad spot. Lucas was his best friend." She sighed. "Anyway, I promised I'd tell you he was really sorry. Don't you still have feelings for him?"

Julia felt a pang of sadness. "Yes, but I don't think it makes any difference. He should have stood by me before. Now it's too late."

173

# Twenty

"**I CAN'T BELIEVE** that we're going to the library on a Saturday," Julia remarked as Kayla jumped into the passenger seat of Julia's Volkswagen. "Especially on one of the only Saturdays that I don't have to go to work."

Kayla laughed, throwing her book bag onto the backseat. "I know it's not the ideal weekend activity. But think of how accomplished we'll feel when we get a head start on our research papers. Besides, you're the one who said that this library has some great books on that George Morandi guy."

Julia smiled. "That's Giorgio Morandi," she corrected her. "I'm cool with doing research as long as we can fit in some fun afterward. Maybe we can hit the music store? I could use some new CDs." She pulled out of Kayla's driveway and turned onto the street.

"Sure," Kayla said. "But I need to get home sort of early. . . . I have a date tonight."

Julia braked at a stop sign. "A date? With

who?" she exclaimed, turning to face Kayla.

Kayla smiled brightly. "Mark Johnston. He's been after me for weeks, and I thought I wasn't interested. But then . . . I don't know, he just kind of grew on me."

"That's awesome!" Julia told her. "It must be nice to have a date," she added, a trifle wistfully.

"You could have one too, if you wanted one." Kayla rolled down her window. "I saw Austin last night at Hot Rods. He asked me to say hello."

"How did he look?" Julia mumbled.

"Oh, let's see," Kayla said thoughtfully. "Eyes to die for, killer smile, great body. Don't tell me just because you haven't talked to him for two weeks that you've forgotten what he looks like."

Julia wrinkled her nose. "Funny, funny. You know what I meant. Did he look happy or sad or what?"

"Not sad . . . but not happy. He definitely didn't have his usual bounce. I guess he seemed kind of preoccupied. He had that same hazy, my-mind-is-somewhere-else look you've been wearing lately."

Julia kept her eyes on the road, not saying anything for a moment. As angry as she was at Austin, she had to admit that she still missed him.

"C'mon, Julia, nobody's perfect," Kayla said, breaking the silence. "Give Austin another chance. At least talk to him."

A sigh escaped Julia's lips. "It's just that I trusted him, and I thought he trusted me. It was such a letdown." She stopped at a red light. "If only he hadn't had to hear the truth from Lucas and Tiffany before he believed me."

Kayla threw up her hands. "You keep saying

that. Maybe Austin *would* have wised up without hearing Lucas's story. But he did hear it. People deserve to be forgiven sometimes, you know."

Julia bit her lip. "I'm just totally confused. It's hard for me to make sense of anything."

"I'll drop it," Kayla said. "But don't write him off yet."

"Okay," Julia said softly. She pulled into the library parking lot. "Here we are."

"I can't wait to hit those books," Kayla teased.

"No kidding." Julia smiled and slammed the car door closed. She got her bag out of the trunk. The two girls walked toward the entrance of the library.

"It's busy for a Saturday," Julia commented when they were inside.

It *was* busy. Julia noticed that there was a fair amount of little kids with parents milling about. Mildred, the same librarian who had helped Julia last time, was at the checkout desk again.

"This librarian's really nice," Julia whispered to Kayla. They walked up to the desk.

"Well, hello there," Mildred greeted them. "You're the one who wanted the Morandi books, right?"

"Right." Julia smiled, surprised she had remembered. "Actually, I came to check them out this time."

"Wonderful," Mildred said. "I'll get them for you. And can I help you, dear?" she asked Kayla.

"I'm looking for some books on Monet," Kayla replied. "By the way, why are there so many kids here today?"

"Oh, we have a story hour on Saturdays here," Mildred explained. "It's just about to start. Normally we have a lovely young lady who reads to the children on Saturdays. But the young man who reads on Tuesdays requested to read today instead."

Julia's heart dropped. *Austin's here today?* She looked at Kayla. "I can't believe he's here . . . now," she whispered.

Kayla squeezed her hand. "I think it's an omen."

"Shall I go get those books for you?" Mildred asked.

"Um . . . ," Julia started.

"That would be great, thank you," Kayla told Mildred. "I think we're going to listen to the story hour first. We'll come pick up the books after."

"All right, dear." Mildred smiled again.

Kayla pulled Julia toward the room where story hour was held.

Julia stopped walking, resisting Kayla. "I don't want to go in there. I don't want to see him."

"I think you do," Kayla said. "I think you'll be surprised."

Julia stared at Kayla, knitting her brow. "What's going on? Do you know something that I don't?"

Kayla shrugged. "Maybe," she teased playfully. She grabbed Julia's hand, pulling her toward the other room once more. "Come on. You won't be disappointed," she promised.

Julia sighed. "You're obviously not going to give up. I don't have much choice."

They walked into the back of the room. Julia took one step in and stopped.

Austin was sitting on a chair, surrounded by a large group of children that was gathered on the floor. He was chatting with a couple of the kids.

*He looks as cute and as sweet today as he did that first day when I saw him here,* Julia thought. But then she reminded herself of the scene at the party—and all of her anger came rushing back.

She turned to Kayla. "This isn't a good idea."

"Just wait," Kayla said mysteriously.

Before Julia could ask Kayla what she meant, she heard Austin start to speak.

Julia looked over at him. He was staring at her with that intense gaze of his, his smile warm and sexy.

"Okay, guys," he said, "*now* we're ready to start." He was still staring at Julia. A couple of the kids turned around to see what he was looking at.

Julia felt herself blushing. "He knew I was going to be here, didn't he?" she whispered to Kayla.

"Maybe. You'll see," Kayla replied. "Just listen."

Austin took his eyes off Julia and picked up a spiral notebook. "This first story is short," he announced. "And it doesn't have any pictures."

A few kids groaned.

"But it's a good one," Austin promised. He opened the notebook and started to read from it. "Once upon a time, there was a beautiful princess named Julia."

Julia gasped. She felt goose bumps prickle her neck as Austin said her name.

Austin looked up at her, catching her eye. Then he looked back down at his notebook and continued to read. "She was the prettiest, smartest, funniest, and most talented princess in the land."

Julia's pulse was racing. She could feel her heart beating faster. Kayla squeezed her arm.

"One day she met a prince named Austin."

"That's your name!" a little girl called out.

"Why, yes, it is." Austin feigned surprise. "What a coincidence!"

Julia couldn't help smiling. Austin glanced at her and smiled back. Then he went on with the story.

"So, of course, Prince Austin immediately fell for Princess Julia—after all, she *was* the most amazing princess in the land. All he wanted to do was to spend time with her. He dreamt about her day and night. And the happiest day of his life was when Princess Julia agreed to go to the Royal Ball with him."

Julia was sure that her cheeks were completely red. "I can't believe this," she said very softly.

"*Now* tell me you won't forgive him," Kayla whispered in her ear.

"Prince Austin and Princess Julia had a wonderful time at the ball," Austin continued. "Lord Lucas and Lady Courtney were also at the ball. They were Prince Austin's oldest friends, and he couldn't wait for them to meet the love of his life, beautiful Princess Julia."

Julia bit her lip.

"But to Prince Austin's surprise, Lord Lucas and Lady Courtney weren't nice to Princess Julia."

"Why not?" a little blond boy in the front asked.

179

"Well, Prince Austin didn't know," Austin explained. "After all, Princess Julia *was* the most wonderful princess. Who wouldn't like her?"

Austin paused, glancing up at Julia again. Julia held his gaze for a moment, then looked down to the ground.

"It turned out that Lord Lucas and Lady Courtney were *jealous* of Princess Julia," Austin went on. "And not only because she was beautiful and smart and talented but also because Prince Austin wanted to spend time with her, instead of with them."

Austin turned the page in the notebook. "One day, Lord Lucas told Prince Austin that Princess Julia was engaged to another prince! Prince Austin was heartbroken. But when he asked Princess Julia about it, she said it wasn't true."

Austin sighed dramatically. "Prince Austin *wanted* to believe her. But Lord Lucas was his oldest friend. He had always looked out for the prince. Lord Lucas used to protect him from dangerous dragons. Prince Austin didn't think that his closest friend would ever lie to him. Princess Julia was furious that Prince Austin didn't believe her, and she refused to ever talk to him again."

Julia felt a lump form in her throat.

"The next couple of weeks were the worst weeks of the prince's life. He was miserable without Princess Julia—she was everything to him. He realized that he had been a fool—that she would never lie and that Lord Lucas actually *did* lie. He was very, very upset with his friend and very, very upset with himself."

Austin closed the notebook. "Now, I'm not sure how this fairy tale ends. There's only one way for this to be a happily-ever-after story."

Austin stared across the room at Julia. She was aware that everyone else in the room was now looking at her too.

She didn't care—she stared back at him, almost in a trance. Her heart was pounding wildly.

"So," Austin said softly, still gazing at Julia, "do you think that after lots of apologies, and lots of begging, the princess eventually forgives the foolish prince?"

"Yes! Yes!" some of the children called out.

But Austin was silent, waiting for Julia's reaction.

Tears had formed in her eyes. Julia gave a small smile and mouthed the word "yes."

Austin broke out into a huge grin. "So the princess forgave the prince, and they rode off on his white horse, into the sunset, happily ever after."

Julia felt warmth rush through her body. She felt like she was in a dream.

"Okay, kids," Austin said, "Sarah's going to read for the rest of story hour." He motioned over to a brown-haired girl in the corner of the room. "I just had to read that story today. I'll see you all on Tuesday."

He stood up and smiled at Julia. He was walking toward her.

Julia turned to Kayla. "Thank you. I know you had to help plan this."

Kayla glowed. "All I did was drag your stubborn self here," she teased. "It was all Austin's idea. Really."

"Wow." Julia sighed happily.

Before she could say anything more, Austin was right in front of her. He touched her arm, and she felt another surge of goose bumps.

"Hi, princess," he said softly.

"Hi," she whispered back.

"Thanks, Kayla," Austin said, only taking his eyes off Julia for a second to look at Kayla.

"My pleasure," Kayla responded. She gave Austin and Julia a playful shove. "Now get lost, you two. Go ride off into the sunset already."

Austin and Julia both laughed. Julia kissed Kayla on the cheek. "Thanks again," she said. "Talk to you later."

"Sure thing." Kayla smiled. "Oh, since you *insisted* on driving, can I please borrow your car to drive home?"

Julia grinned. "Of course. Here." She handed Kayla the keys to her VW. "Let's go," she said to Austin.

Austin took her hand in his, and they walked out of the room, then out of the library.

Neither of them said anything as they reached the parking lot. Julia was basking in the moment. Suddenly everything felt right again. She knew she could forgive him now.

They walked up to Austin's Camaro. *The white horse,* Julia thought, smiling.

Austin bent down and kissed her on the lips lightly, gently. Then he pulled her to him, holding her tight. "I was afraid I'd lost you for good," he said in a choked voice. "I'm so sorry. I'm sorry I ever doubted you."

"Don't say anything else," Julia told him in a hoarse whisper. "Just hold me close."

*Do you ever wonder about falling in love? About members of the opposite sex? Do you need a little friendly advice but have no one to turn to? Well, that's where we come in . . . Jenny and Jake. Send us those questions you're dying to ask, and we'll give you the straight scoop on life and love in the nineties.*

## DEAR JAKE

**Q:** *I have this friend, Jeremy, who I spend a lot of time with in school. We're in many of the same clubs, and we have similar interests. The problem is his girlfriend. She's really jealous even though he and I are just friends and neither of us wants more. How can I get her to understand that I'm not interested in him and to leave me alone?*

*AR, Prattville, AL*

**A:** I'm sure it's frustrating to have this girl suspect you of something you're innocent of. However, I must admit that she might have a reason to be jealous. Even if your feelings are strictly friendly, Jeremy's might not be. Guys don't usually get that close to girls unless they are at least a little attracted to them. Maybe his girlfriend notices something that you're not seeing. On top of that, maybe you feel more for this guy than you even realize. Make sure that you have it straight in your head exactly what you want.

If you know that this is just a friendship for

both of you, then his girlfriend is the only one with a problem. He has a right to have female friends, and she has to live with that. In order to get her to leave you alone and to also be sure that Jeremy understands that you guys are just friends, ask him to clear things up with his girlfriend.

Q: *I have a crush on this guy, and I think he likes me too. I even think he knows that I like him, but he hasn't done anything about it. How can I get him to ask me out?*

KC, Jackson, MS

A: I'm going to let you in on a little secret about guys: We're not always aware of as much as you think we are. So even if you *think* this guy knows how you feel, it's possible that he's clueless.

You have two options. You could consider making the first move yourself. Guys love it when you take the pressure off by letting us know you're interested. Try suggesting a movie he mentioned wanting to see. If you're just not comfortable with that, then give him some more obvious signs that you like him. He's probably shy and needs some reassurance that you won't reject him if he asks you out. If you don't want things to keep going like they are now, you'll have to take matters into your own hands one way or another.

# DEAR JENNY

**Q:** *I've liked this guy named Jeff since I was in seventh grade, but he never seemed to notice me. Now I'm in tenth grade, and I'm going out with another guy, Aaron. I like Aaron a lot, but I still have feelings for Jeff, and Jeff is finally starting to flirt with me. I'm so confused. What should I do?*

**MB, Madison, WI**

**A:** The first thing you need to decide is whether or not Jeff is really interested in a relationship with you. A lot of people flirt for fun, without having any real feelings. Perhaps he is flirting with you because he knows you have a boyfriend and he just wants to start trouble. Or maybe it took your relationship with Aaron to make him realize how he really feels about you. You have to watch how Jeff reacts to you both when Aaron is around and when he isn't.

If you are sure that there is a choice to be made, then you have to think very carefully about your feelings. It's easy to be swayed by the past, and it can be very flattering to have a boy show interest in you after you've liked him for so long. If you choose Jeff, it must not be for these reasons but because he is the person you want to be with *now*. Aaron has made you happy when Jeff wasn't around, and you can't forget that. In the end, you'll have to listen to your heart and let it tell you who to choose.

**Q:** *Adam and I have been going out for about a year now, and I really love him. The only problem is that he likes to joke around a lot and call me names. Sometimes he'll even tell me he hates me. I know he doesn't mean it, but I'm getting tired of hearing it and he won't stop. My friends think I should dump him, but I don't know. Are they right?*

**KG, Harrisonburg, VA**

**A:** You say that you love Adam, but it doesn't sound like you're happy with the relationship. Have you told him how much all the things he says hurt you? Perhaps he really loves you too and he's just not as mature as you are, so he hides behind these jokes and insults. Tell him that he's upsetting you. If he actually tries to change, then you know he means well.

If he keeps saying these things, then it's time to listen to your friends. They love you and they have your best interests at heart. They're sick of watching you get hurt, and you should be sick of hurting. You deserve better.

*Do you have questions about love? Write to:*

Jenny Burgess or Jake Korman
c/o Daniel Weiss Associates
33 West 17th Street
New York, NY 10011